My undying love and appreciation to Lin, Gu, Sarah, Annie and Jane for putting up with all the time spent lost in the tunnels of my mind.

About the Author

Saxon Bennett lives in the East Mountains of New Mexico. She is an avid lover of red and green as long as it comes on the side. She still pursues various forms of sporting extremism with a healthy disregard for the onset of middle age—always be nice to your elders, you'll be there one day.

Chapter One

Hilton Withers pulled up in front of her old Victorian house in Seattle's university district. It was pale yellow with a faded red shingle roof. The house needed a paint job and the yard was a mess. Hilton ignored these facts. Her pea-green Volkswagen bug barely squeezed into what was left of the driveway. It was Friday night and the house was filled with Queer Nation people and who-ever else wanted to come. This was party zone central. Shannon, her great white Pyrenees, licked her lips, having just finished her McDonald's cheeseburger. It was her Friday night treat.

"You know, those things are bad for you," Hilton told her.

Shannon barked.

"I know I do bad things too."

Shannon licked Hilton's face.

"Ick! I find leftover burger juice offensive."

Shannon barked again and her black lips curled up in a smile. Hilton laughed. People who did not know animals would think her crazy to believe a dog could smile and have opinions, but Hilton was convinced that Shannon was more intuitive than most of the women she knew. She kept this information to herself.

Hilton and Shannon went around back and nearly tripped over a couple of shaved-headed, seriously pierced women fornicating in the wisteria bushes alongside the house. They were stepping all over the Japanese peonies. It was going to be one of those nights, Hilton thought as she unlocked the door to her garden cottage. Set back twenty yards from the house, the cottage had once served as the mother-in-law quarters. It had large lead-paned windows on all four sides. When the long burgundy velvet curtains were open Hilton felt like she was living in a giant fishbowl. The cottage was surrounded by her grandmother's overgrown rose garden. Gran had died two years ago and ever since then everything had slid into a steady decline. Every once in a while, Hilton would get a wild hair up her ass and do a bit of trimming. The entire backyard was overgrown and it had occurred to her to hire a gardener but she wasn't certain she could handle the commitment.

She unlocked the door and Shannon bounded through it and jumped up on the king-size waterbed.

"Be careful," Hilton warned. The waterbed, complete with a velour comforter, was a throwback to her teenage years. She was hard put to part with it. The mattress had been patched several times due to Shannon's exuberant leaps. A hundred-and-twenty-pound ball of fur with huge toenails was not a waterbed's best friend. Hilton told herself when the mattress flooded the place she'd buy a new bed.

She wondered if this was a holdover attitude she had gleaned from her grandmother along with the house mantra, "Follow the straight and narrow." As a child Hilton had looked for straight and narrow pathways thinking this was what her grandmother meant. Her grandmother, Nettie Ella Withers, had grown up during the Great Depression. At the age of thirteen she had started selling pickles on the streets of Seattle during those lean years before FDR put the whole country on the dole, as her grandmother put it. She grew the cucumbers, saved the seeds, perfected the recipe and went on to make more money than her son, Percy, or grandchild, Hilton, would ever need. Hilton hated pickles and so did her grandmother. There was never a jar of Withers Homegrown Pickles in the house. Despite all this money, Gran never threw anything away until it had completely exhausted its lifespan. Hilton pondered whether she was subscribing to this doctrine when it came to the waterbed.

Shannon whined.

"Oh, get over it," Hilton said, rubbing Shannon's soft ears.

Hilton rustled around in her closet for something to wear. Finding nothing she liked she was forced to rummage around the cottage. She found a pile of clean T-shirts neatly folded on the countertop of the kitchenette that took up one wall of the small cottage. Her roommate Liz must have taken pity on her and done some laundry. She never used the kitchenette although it did have a small gas stove and an old porcelain sink. She had installed a stainless steel dorm fridge. The cottage was basically one big room with a bathroom off the kitchenette. Hilton had taken up residence in the cottage after Gran died because the big house, which Gran had left to her, had become too populated with parties, activist planning groups and all-night study cram sessions.

Digging through the pile she opted for a black T-shirt that said Teach Masturbation and a pair of camouflage shorts. She gazed longingly at the claw-footed porcelain tub. The pipes were so corroded that she would be collecting Social Security before the tub filled enough to take a bath. She scooped up her clothes and told Shannon to stay. The house would be too crowded and she was an overprotective parent. Shannon put her head down on the side rail of the bed and looked perfectly pitiful.

"I won't be gone long," Hilton said as she slipped out the cottage door. Shannon barked once to indicate her displeasure and then Hilton knew she'd settle down for a nap. That was one of the things she liked about her dog—she was predictable, unlike most of the other creatures in her life.

Hilton snuck in the back door of the house, through the kitchen, which was only mildly populated, and up the back stairs of the house. The back stairs had once been used as the servants' entrance to the rest of the house. The other set of stairs with its dark oak railings and balustrade had been used solely by the family members unless the maid was dusting it. There was no cleaning staff now but Hilton still preferred the back way.

The old Victorian house had three proper stories and then the attic. Each floor had its own bathroom, all in various states of disrepair. Her three roommates each had a bedroom and a bath on one of three floors. This allowed all of them some privacy and more than enough space as there was a sunroom on the third floor and several smaller storage rooms and various alcoves spread throughout the house. The house was actually quite large although they didn't use that much of it anymore. She was hoping to make it to the third-floor bathroom, which was in the best state of repair, without being noticed by anyone, including her girlfriend, Natalie.

Natalie was currently infatuated with someone new and Hilton always had trouble with these liaisons. Although there had been plenty of them, they still bothered her. This one's name was Sherry and she was a biker chick. Hilton felt totally inadequate in dealing with this one. With most of Natalie's girlfriends she had a chance of outshining them, but aside from donning leathers and buying a Harley she was out of luck. She was almost to the second-story landing when Nat caught up with her.

"I brought you a beer and something special," Nat said. She handed Hilton a bottle of Rolling Rock and a hit of ecstasy. "It's a little something to take the nip off the day."

Hilton scowled.

Nat kissed her cheek. "Lighten up."

"She's coming tonight," Hilton said, knowing it was more a statement than a question.

"Who?"

"Don't play with me." Hilton studied Nat's face, trying to read what was written there. Nat was a petite woman, with short brown hair, pretty blue eyes and a pirate's smile. It was times like these that Hilton suffered from what she called her caveman complex. She wanted to lift Nat up on her shoulders and carry her off somewhere safe where they could live their lives out in quiet seclusion. Nat was in her last year of college. The only reason she was going to college was to get her rather substantial trust fund. She had to graduate to collect. Nat had chosen her major accordingly. She was studying art history because, as she put it, "All you have to do is memorize paintings and dates. I can do that." That was Nat's basic philosophy on life. Do as little as you can to get most of what you want.

"Sherry's coming tonight and I just wanted to warn you," Nat said. She didn't meet Hilton's gaze.

"Just don't bang her in front of me," Hilton said. She clenched the Ecstasy in her coiled hand.

"We're not doing that." This time Nat looked at her.

"Not yet," Hilton said, turning to leave.

When she got upstairs, she ran the bath and deposited the Ecstasy in an empty dark brown bottle of hydrogen peroxide with all the other pills. Hilton had a stash to be envied. She should really flush them but they served as a testimony to all the times Nat had wanted her pacified. Nat was a lot like the shrinks Hilton had seen while she was growing up who always thought she needed drugs to lessen her intensity and dilute her personality, to make her into somebody else.

She also kept the pills as part of a revenge fantasy she had going. One day she would take all those pills to Olympia and stash them in her father's medicine cabinet, then she'd tip off the *National Inquirer*. Her father's political career as a senator was squeaky clean except for his gay daughter and dead wife. Through the years, Hilton had come up with elaborate revenge scenarios as a payback for being made an orphan.

Hilton slipped into the bath and thought about the one and only adult conversation she and Gran had had about her mother. Gran told her that her father, Percy, was a horrible prick who had killed the one beautiful thing in his life, her mother. Gran loved Hilton's mother, Louise, like the daughter she'd never had. When Louise died at age twenty-eight, Gran snatched Hilton and told Percy if he had any ideas of fighting for custody, she'd cut him off without a penny. Percy was just beginning his political career and needed the money.

By the time Gran died, all Hilton remembered about her father was that day on the beach when they found her mother drowned. Now, he viewed her as a political liability despite the fact that she retained the keys to the family fortune. Gran had cut him out of the will. This did little for any hope of reconciliation.

Hilton finished bathing and got dressed. When she came downstairs the party was in full swing. The stereo was blasting techno tunes and the living room had become a dance floor. Hilton scanned the crowd for Nat. She was nowhere to be found. Someone touched her arm. It was Liz.

"She went for a ride with Sherry," Liz said.

"Great." Hilton made her way through the crowd to the kitchen for another beer. Liz followed her. Hilton offered perfunctory greetings to the women she knew. Most of them were Nat's friends. She always thought of that Counting Crows song with the line, "I don't know anyone at the party, but I'm always the host."

"Are you all right with this?" Liz asked as Hilton poked around in the fridge for another beer, which was like a world tour of beers, all of them left from other parties. She chose two Red Stripes. Tonight, they would go to Jamaica.

Hilton handed Liz a beer.

"Thanks."

"All right with what?" Hilton asked. She took a sip of beer. It was ice cold. It had obviously been in there for a while.

"You know."

"Isn't this the tenth or eleventh time?"

"I lost count," Liz replied.

Hilton watched Liz pick at the label on the beer bottle. It was a favorite tactic of hers to avoid eye contact when something uncomfortable came up. Liz was very protective of Hilton and if she had any brains she'd dump Nat and date Liz. She had met Liz in her computer programming class. She was a tall, dark-haired, long-legged beauty from Missouri. She had moved to Seattle to go to graduate school. Her longtime lover had dumped her rather abruptly upon their arrival and left her destitute. The lover owned the pocketbook. Hilton took her into her home. "Hilton's home for wayward women," Liz liked to joke. Gran had been adamant about philanthropy and Hilton had taken it to a more personal level. Liz had been there two years and was on the verge of graduating.

"The label's painted on, so you'll just have to talk to me face-to-face," Hilton said, reaching out and lifting Liz's chin. She had long, chestnut brown hair and the most amazing blue eyes. She was wearing a pair of khaki shorts and a white blouse. She looked like the all-American college girl and Hilton couldn't help wondering how she'd come to be part of this dysfunctional group.

"All right, it's twelve. There was the plumber, remember?"

"Oh, that's right. I had forgotten about the plumber. That's why my tub doesn't work and the toilet still runs."

"Exactly."

Jessie came up to them breathless. "Liz, I think I've found you the perfect girlfriend."

"I can only imagine," Hilton said, watching as mortification danced across Liz's face.

"There's no such thing," Liz said.

"No, look, she's sitting right over there on the couch," Jessie said, pointing to a blond woman with a teddy bear sitting on her lap. Jessie was another one of Hilton's roommates. She was a complete nymphomaniac and was instantly in love with anyone who went to bed with her. Jessie was cute. She had spiky, black hair, olive skin and sparkling green eyes. She spent a lot of time at the gym, mostly in search of prey, but had a nice body as an accidental consequence of going there five days a week. She had a job as the receptionist and towel girl. She was trying to get her phys ed degree so she could be a trainer. Unfortunately, studying was never a priority with Jessie so she often had to drop classes and then retake them.

"What's with the bear?" Hilton asked.

"She's her constant companion. Her first lover gave it to her and the bear's been with her ever since."

"Where's the girlfriend?" Liz asked.

"Oh, long gone, but if you talk nice to the bear you're in like Flynn," Jessie said.

"Let me guess, the bear's name is Amelia Bearheart," Liz said. She finished her beer. Hilton noticed she'd still managed to scrape off part of the painted label. She put the bottle down and was digging white paint from underneath her fingernail.

"How'd you know? See, you're halfway there," Jessie said, obviously impressed with Liz's ability to name bears.

"The bear's got a flight jacket on and goggles," Hilton said, having reached the same conclusion.

"Why aren't you going after her?" Liz asked.

"I want her friend, the tall blonde over there," Jessie replied.

"Oh, so I'm supposed to entertain the freak with the bear while you cruise her friend," Liz said snidely.

"Well, I mean, it would help. Couldn't you just go and talk to her?"

"No." Liz left to get another beer.

"What's up with her? The woman looks nice."

"I gotta go," Hilton said.

"Where are you going?" Jessie asked.

"To check on Shannon. I'll be back and then I'll talk to the freak while you line up your next conquest."

"Really?"

"What are friends for."

Jessie smiled and disappeared back into the crowd.

Hilton went out back to discover that Shannon had gotten out and was playing ball with a woman she had never seen before. She must not have closed the door tight. Shannon was pretty good at nudging the door open if there was half a chance she might be successful at escaping. She always stayed in the yard but she seemed to do it as a protest that she'd been left behind. Shannon came romping up to her.

"Is she your dog?" the woman asked.

"Yes, and she's supposed to be in the cottage taking a nap right now," Hilton said. Shannon rolled over as if to apologize. Hilton sat on the grass next to her and rubbed her soft white belly.

"Oh, so she's a fugitive. Hi, my name's Emily. I'm your new neighbor. Jessie invited me over but it was a little too crowded inside, so I thought I might get some air."

"Well, it's nice to meet you. I'm Hilton."

"You're the pickle heiress."

"I love that introduction. Jessie told you that."

"Yes, I'm sorry. I've never met a pickle heiress before."

"Am I everything you imagined?"

"That and more," Emily said coyly.

Hilton smiled. The woman was obviously flirting with her, and for once Hilton didn't mind. Emily had dyed pink hair and was wearing cutoffs and a man's undershirt with no bra. Both her nipples were pierced and she had nice, small round breasts. She was nothing Hilton would normally date.

"So are you from here?" Hilton asked politely. She sat down on the porch steps next to her. She'd rather talk to a punk rocker than a woman with a teddy bear as a constant companion. Jessie would get over it.

"No, I just moved here from Vancouver. I'm going to school."

"What for?" Hilton took the last swig of her beer and wished she'd grabbed another one on the way out. Emily was also out of beer, she noticed.

"I don't know yet. I'm still doing basic courses right now. I must've changed majors five times now. It's hard trying to decide what you want to do with your life. I'll probably just get a bachelor's in liberal arts and then slave away in a coffee shop somewhere."

Hilton laughed. "Hey, do you want to get another beer?"

"Sure."

"I've got a private stash in the cottage. We could avoid the crowd."

"Great," Emily said. She followed Hilton and Shannon back to the cottage. Emily sat on the bed because the only two chairs in the place were old cracked leather wingbacks where Hilton stacked her records.

Hilton watched to see if having to sit on the bed made Emily uncomfortable. Obviously not, she thought as Emily kicked her shoes off, fluffed up one of the big pillows at the headboard and looked around inquisitively.

"My, you're quite the collector," Emily said, taking the Corona beer that Hilton offered her.

"Got any requests?" Hilton asked, kneeling in front of the record player.

Emily put her forefinger to her lips and appeared to be lost in a quick search of her mental files. Hilton waited, wondering what she'd come up with. She seldom met anyone whose musical tastes even bordered on eclectic. Most people, even Nat, simply chose the latest tunes, which meant Hilton had to resort to CDs to fulfill the request. She preferred records. She liked the scratchy sounds and the feel of vinyl as she put them on the player.

"How about Van Morrison's 'Brown-Eyed Girl,' Patsy Cline's 'Three Cigarettes' and maybe a little Bob Marley, 'No Woman No Cry.'"

"Music lover, eh?"

"Avid," she said, sitting up on the bed and crossing her legs. She took a sip of beer.

Maybe tonight wasn't going to be so bad after all, Hilton thought as she put on Emily's first request.

❧

They spent the next four hours listening to songs and drinking beer. They had ordered pizza and now Hilton was looking in the fridge for more beer. "I could go foraging in the house," she offered, not relishing the idea.

"No, stay here. I think I've exceeded my daily limit anyway. You might disappear into the crowded void of your house party and I'll never see again."

Hilton laughed. For the first time in weeks she felt relaxed. She looked over at Shannon, who was sleeping peacefully in the corner. "So what's next?" Hilton asked innocently.

"I'd really like to kiss you," Emily said.

Before Hilton had time to protest, Emily had taken Hilton's face in her hands and kissed her ardently. Emily's soft lips brushed against hers and her tongue was doing the most amazing things. Hilton wasn't certain she would have protested anyway. What little resolve she may have had died away as Emily pulled up her T-shirt and kissed her stomach. Emily ran her tongue just under the waistband of Hilton's shorts. She tugged at the button and looked up at Hilton.

"Please," Hilton said, feeling a shiver run through her.

Emily undid the button and zipper and pulled her shorts off. She ran her finger down the center of Hilton's underwear and parted her lips gently. Hilton moaned. Emily pulled her underwear off. Hilton thought of Nat for three seconds as Emily took her in her mouth, inserting her tongue and sort of fucking her. Hilton didn't know if her thought of Natalie was guilt or revenge.

When Emily rolled her over and took her from behind she had completely forgotten about Nat. Hilton arched up to meet Emily's fingers. Emily had taken off her shirt and Hilton could feel her breasts as they met her back. They rocked against each other.

"Is this good?" Emily asked as she ground against her.

"Fabulous," Hilton said. She couldn't hold herself a moment longer. Her orgasm shot through her like a lightning storm coursing through her veins. She gasped and lay still for a moment. She could feel her own jagged breath in unison with Emily's.

"That was nice," Emily said, rolling off her and scooping her up in her arms.

"Very nice," Hilton murmured, her face buried between Emily's soft breasts. She licked the beads of sweat that lay there.

Emily pulled off her shorts and rolled Hilton on her back. She slid her thigh between Hilton's leg. Hilton could feel her wetness.

"Come here." She pulled Emily on top of her. Hilton tugged at Emily's nipple rings. Emily leaned in toward her and Hilton sucked her nipple and the nipple ring. She could feel Emily shudder. "You like?"

"Oh, yes," Emily said, offering up her other breast. She kept rocking toward Hilton with her breasts while Hilton nipped and suckled them. Hilton cupped her hand between Emily's leg and thrust her fingers inside. Emily moaned and then ground against Hilton's hand. "Oh, just like that."

Hilton thought there was nothing quite so erotic as watching a cute girl move against you as you ran your hand across her breasts. Hilton knew it would be the wee hours of the morning before Emily would leave.

BACK TALK

Saxon Bennett

Bella
BOOKS

2006

Bella Books, Inc.
P.O. Box 10543
Tallahassee, FL 32302

Printed in the United States of America on acid-free paper
First Edition

Editor: Christi Cassidy
Cover designer: Sandy Knowles

ISBN 1-59493-028-7

"That was nice," Emily said, rolling off her and scooping her up in her arms.

"Very nice," Hilton murmured, her face buried between Emily's soft breasts. She licked the beads of sweat that lay there.

Emily pulled off her shorts and rolled Hilton on her back. She slid her thigh between Hilton's leg. Hilton could feel her wetness.

"Come here." She pulled Emily on top of her. Hilton tugged at Emily's nipple rings. Emily leaned in toward her and Hilton sucked her nipple and the nipple ring. She could feel Emily shudder. "You like?"

"Oh, yes," Emily said, offering up her other breast. She kept rocking toward Hilton with her breasts while Hilton nipped and suckled them. Hilton cupped her hand between Emily's leg and thrust her fingers inside. Emily moaned and then ground against Hilton's hand. "Oh, just like that."

Hilton thought there was nothing quite so erotic as watching a cute girl move against you as you ran your hand across her breasts. Hilton knew it would be the wee hours of the morning before Emily would leave.

Visit

Bella Books

at

BellaBooks.com

or call our toll-free number

1-800-729-4992

Chapter Two

Early Saturday morning, Anne Counterman sat frowning at her computer screen. She was attempting to create an interactive Web site for her radio program, "Back Talk." She swore that they, being management, had given her the lamest person they could find to be her Webmaster. "Web-make-a-mess-master is more like it," she grumbled.

She moved in disgust away from her site and began perusing the sites of the other radio programs that existed under the conglomerate of Argonaut Airways. She came to a site for one of the smaller FM stations. It was marvelous.

"Now, that's more like it," she said. She clicked on her speakerphone and called Ed Marcy, her program director. He also put in a few hours on Saturday mornings in the peace and quiet of a place almost vacant except for the FM stations who had young jocks spinning tunes and advertisements. They didn't require the research and the phone power that the talk shows needed. The weekends were always a welcome break from the frenetic pace they normally operated under. "Ed, are you busy?" she asked over the speakerphone.

"Never too busy for you, Anne," Ed answered, his gruff voice laced with an unnatural sweetness.

Anne smiled. "Ed, you're so full of shit."

He laughed. "I am. What do you need?"

"A new Webmaster," she said, scrolling down through the Web site. This stuff is good, she thought.

"Gee, is that all?"

"Come see this Web site," Anne said.

Ed groaned. "Like I need some exercise."

"Ed, come on."

"My doctor will thank you," he said. Anne could hear the squeak of his desk chair as he hoisted himself out of it.

When he arrived he peered over her shoulder. "Now, that is a good site."

"Whose is it?" Anne asked, leaning back in her chair. Her shoulders ached and something in her neck cracked. It was time to go to the chiropractor and have him straighten her out again.

"It's Hilton's."

"Whose?"

"She's an intern," Ed said, digging his hand into Anne's candy jar. He pulled out a sour apple Jolly Rancher, unwrapped it and popped it in his mouth.

"As in, unpaid intern?" Anne queried. This was going to be easier than she thought. Over the years she had become a pretty good headhunter, unscrupulously appropriating the best help from wherever she found it. In the radio business there wasn't time or resources to be frittered away on waiting to get what you wanted. You had to go out and grab it.

"Yep, how they get people to do that I'll never know. You couldn't get me to pick up a paper clip without a paycheck."

Anne watched as he maneuvered the candy in his mouth. "Did you get that tooth fixed yet?"

"No, that would require going to the dentist. I'll just wait until it abscesses and I'm in incredible pain and then I'll go."

Anne laughed. "Good idea. I mean, prevention is so banal."

"I can get Hilton in here if you want to talk to her," he offered.

That was one of the things Anne liked about Ed. He knew how to read her and could almost sense her motivations before she had them.

Ed dug in the candy jar for another Jolly Rancher.

"I could be interested in talking to her," Anne said coyly.

"Yeah, I bet you would." Ed winced and looked around. Anne pulled her waste can from under her desk. Ed plucked the candy from his mouth and deposited it.

"Sometimes we have to acknowledge our limitations. I'll get Gummy Bears next time and you can swear off hard candy. It won't make you a lesser man."

Ed smiled. "For the guy with bad teeth."

Anne laughed. She liked Ed. He was one of the few people who didn't pity her or think it was intrinsically her fault that her ex-husband left her for a swank uptown lawyer named Phil. Ed had simply said, "It's his loss." Ed looked like a Franciscan friar with his graying ring of hair and his shiny bald spot on top on his round head, but his brilliant blue eyes and sleek nose gave him the air of an aristocrat. He was capable of speaking in high Latin and the latest street lingo. If he wore a frock instead of khaki Dockers and a blue oxford with no tie he could have walked out of the *Canterbury Tales* with complete credibility.

"I'll call her."

"Ed, it's Saturday."

"The Web site is her baby. She'll come. Do you know who she is?"

"Hilton, the computer whiz kid?" Anne ventured.

"Hilton Withers," Ed said.

Anne could tell he was waiting for her response but she didn't have one. She raised her eyebrows in anticipation and waited.

Ed gave up. "Senator Percy Withers' estranged, lesbian, pickle heiress daughter."

"What the hell is she doing here?"

"Rumor has it she likes your show."

"I've got a shoo-in then," Anne said, scrolling through the Web site again. She felt her mood improving. She liked getting her way and now she knew Ed was going to help her. This was even better. He didn't always go along with her ideas but when he did they usually turned out for the best. Ed was her thermometer when it came to her career, telling her what was hot and what ran cold. She supposed program directors were supposed to have a knack for that but Ed seemed to have more than that. He appeared to be gifted in that department.

"I'd say so, but wait until you meet her. She's an odd duck." Ed picked up the phone and then rummaged around in his pocket for a small tattered notebook where he kept all his secret numbers. He could get ahold of anyone at anytime. Anne wasn't certain how he got this information, whether he threatened the removal of toenails for private cell phone numbers and pagers or if he refused to hire you if you didn't give him complete access to every phone line in your possession. One corner of the pad looked like it had been dipped in ketchup, and all the edges had what Anne referred to as finger juice, that oily grime that too much contact with skin gave to inanimate objects. He began fingering through it until he found what he was looking for.

"What do you mean?"

"Well, first off, there's the dog. If you hire her, her dog, Shannon, comes with."

"To work? Isn't there some building code against that?"

"Actually not. Ever heard of Petsmart?" Ed said, smiling.

Anne gave this some thought. Her insurance agent brought her cat to work. So it must be all right. Anne could tell he was waiting for her to pull out. It was probably some little fluffy thing that liked a biscuit now and then and slept the rest of the day. "We all have our little idiosyncrasies."

"Hilton takes the cake." Ed dialed the number.

Twenty minutes later, Hilton Withers and her dog were standing in Ed's office. Anne sat casually lounging in Ed's waiting room while he told Hilton what was going on. The fluffy little thing Anne had envisioned turned out to be a massive white dog with a head as big as a soccer ball. She did appear to be well-behaved as she sat quietly by Hilton's side. He had led her to believe there was something up with the Web site and now Anne could tell Hilton was not happy about the turn of events. Ed's office had a picture window on one side. Hilton's back was turned so she couldn't see Anne. Having spent years behind a glass partition doing the radio show had given her the ancillary gift of reading lips. Anne was reading Ed's lips. Hilton, it appeared, didn't feel properly dressed. She was attempting to straighten out her wrinkled white shirt by tucking it in a pair of faded camouflage shorts. She pulled her shoulder-length hair back into a ponytail.

Hilton was a very pretty young woman with perfectly straight blond hair and blue eyes. She was thin and looked younger than her twenty-something years. So she's rich and pretty and thin, Anne thought. In the eyes of the world this meant she had everything, not to mention she was smart. It doesn't get any better, Anne smirked to herself.

So Hilton was uncomfortable. She would put her at ease. Anne enjoyed making people squirm, using others to do her dirty work so that she could come in and become the breast of comfort.

Anne knew just when to make her entrance. She walked into Ed's office nonchalantly.

"You must be Hilton," Anne said, extending her hand. Hilton looked startled.

"Yes, Ed was telling me that you liked the Web site." Hilton shook her hand.

Anne noticed that she only made eye contact for a brief moment. This meant she was shy and shy people were seldom arrogant, Anne thought.

"I absolutely love it. Have you seen my current one?"

"Well, of course," Hilton said.

Shannon was sniffing Anne's shoe. Hilton snapped her fingers and Shannon reluctantly returned to her side. She let out a heavy sigh.

"What do you think of it?" Anne asked, leaning on the corner of Ed's desk.

Hilton looked over at Ed as if looking for clues. "Tell her the truth," he said. He folded his arms across his chest and grinned big. Hilton must have taken this for a sign.

"Honestly?" Hilton asked. She reached down to pet Shannon, who had been nuzzling her.

"Please," Anne said. She stuck her hand out so Shannon could smell it.

"It sucks."

Anne and Ed both burst out laughing.

"What I mean is that it could use some work. Your show is so vibrant and funny and the Web site is so bland in comparison. Bart is not your man."

"Boy, you can say that again," Anne said. She rubbed Shannon's ears and Anne could tell being nice to the dog scored big points with Hilton. Anne liked dogs. She'd had them growing up and then once college and career came along there didn't seem time to care for one.

"Anne was thinking that you might like to give it a shot," Ed said.

"Really?" Hilton asked.

"Really. Have you had breakfast?" Anne said, liking that Hilton was excited.

"No, I just got up, like, twenty minutes ago and it's only eight-thirty."

"Let's go eat and we'll talk," Anne said.

"That'd be great."

"Does Shannon have a favorite place?" Anne asked.

"McDonald's," Hilton said.

"That sounds wonderful, and then we'll take it to the park,"

Anne said, knowing for certain dogs were not allowed in restaurants.

Shannon obviously had a vocabulary because she barked and jumped up on Hilton, nearly flooring her.

"Whoa, girl. Yes, we're going."

They walked past Anne's studio on the way to the elevators. "Hey, do you want to see the studio?" Anne asked.

"Sure," Hilton said.

Anne unlocked the door. Her boots made noise on the wood floors. Shannon went over and sniffed the leather couch that lined one wall. Two chairs and a coffee table finished off the reception area. To one side was a semi-circular desk. "That's Veronica's area. She's our producer."

"Nice studio," Hilton commented.

"And this is the control room," Anne said, leading her into the large glass booth that housed the equipment necessary to run the program. It had an octagonal desk with the control board in the middle, a switchboard for the phones on one side and computer desk on the other. "I thought we could put you here. That way you could observe the show and between you and Dave, our broadcast engineer, work something out with the Web site."

"That sounds great," Hilton said. "Wow, a D-eight-hundred." She touched the control board.

"So you know a little more than just the computer stuff," Anne said.

"Not really, I'm just fascinated by electronics."

"I'm sure Dave will give you the rundown on everything."

They exited the control room. "And then over here is my booth," Anne said. She watched as Hilton went to one of the two large windows located on both sides of the soundproof booth.

"Great view," Hilton said.

Anne came over and took it in with her. The earlier drizzle of the day had cleared up and she could see the Space Needle and just barely perceptible was the tip of Mount Rainier. "Boy, you don't see that very often."

"No, it's gorgeous."

"Is this acceptable?" Anne asked. She could tell Shannon liked it. She was sprawled out on the wood floor underneath the slow-running overhead fan.

"Oh, yeah."

"Let's go get breakfast then."

Shannon stood up immediately. Anne smiled. She liked the dog.

Later that afternoon, Anne was sitting on her back patio gloating over her latest success at headhunting. Hilton had eagerly jumped at the chance to become a paid Webmistress for Anne's show. It wasn't much of a theft because interns came to radio stations in hopes of finding full-time employment. The sister station where Hilton worked would easily find a replacement as the list of applicants for internships was endless. Hilton needed at least a week of just observing the program before she went to work reformatting the Web site. Anne poured herself a glass of horribly expensive Pinot Noir. Sometimes it felt good to be her.

She was still gloating when Gerald let himself in the back gate. There were times when it bothered her that he still felt so free to wander about her house, but she supposed she could handle it. He had lived there for five years, been responsible for the decorating and landscaping and then given it all to her when they divorced. Still, it was an invasion of privacy, and what if someday she was spending the afternoon doing a little hanky-panky with a new heartthrob. It would be embarrassing if her ex-husband came cruising in. She could change the locks but somehow that seemed an act of hostility and she didn't want that. There wouldn't be any liaisons anytime soon, so what did it really matter?

"I thought I'd find you out back," Gerald Parsing said, flopping his six-foot frame into the yellow wooden chair. He brushed his errant brown forelock out of his eyes and looked at her inquisitively.

"I was just relaxing."

"And?" he asked, picking up the bottle of wine Anne had sitting next to her. He examined the label. "We must be celebrating something."

"As a matter of fact we are. I just snagged a really good Webmistress who's going to do wonders for my new site."

"Doing a little headhunting?"

"It's a dog-eat-dog world out there. Did you want a glass?"

"Sure."

Anne went into the kitchen and got him a glass. It was Waterford crystal and had been one of their wedding presents. She really had walked off with the store. She went back outside to find him plucking some of the dead leaves off one of the rosebushes he had laboriously planted alongside the patio.

"The roses are coming along nicely." He sat back down and took the glass of wine she offered him.

"Why don't you take some home for Philip?"

"That would be nice. He would take it as a peace offering," Gerald said.

"A sign that I no longer harbor any ill will for stealing my husband."

"Anne . . ."

She gazed into his dark blue eyes. She couldn't honestly say that she didn't feel pain when she looked at him. They had been the perfect couple and everyone thought theirs was a marriage that would last. They had similar interests. So she thought for five years. They had agreed children were not really imminent in their plans. They both liked to travel; they enjoyed their careers and hobbies. It seemed they were madly in love. And then one day Gerald came home and told her he was in love with another man. If anything can make a woman feel inadequate it's being replaced by someone you have no hope of competing with. Phil had a penis and she didn't. It was hopeless. She kept hoping one day she would find humor in this. That day had yet to arrive. "Gerald, what went wrong?"

"It's not you. It's not anything you did. It was me."

21

"No, it was Philip." Anne poured herself another glass of wine.

"It would've happened sooner or later. I came to invite you to a barbeque," he said, pointedly changing the subject.

"So I can hang out with a bunch of gay people. I'm sure I'll find a date that way. No, thanks."

"You never know," Gerald said, finishing his glass of wine. "I worry about you, Anne. I want you to be happy."

"I'm fine. Besides, I'm supposed to have dinner with my parents tonight."

"Oh, goody."

Anne laughed. "Don't you miss those family dinners where my father keeps quiet while my mother meddles in your business. She still thinks I drove you to this."

"I know. I'm sorry. I should call her."

"No, don't. The longer you stay away the closer she'll get to letting it go."

"All right. I should go."

"Tell Phil hello for me."

"I will. He feels bad, you know." Gerald didn't meet her gaze. Instead, he went and picked a single yellow rose.

"I'm sure he does," Anne said. *Like, everytime he holds you in his arms.* She tried to imagine Philip falling down on his knees in penance to a righteous God and begging forgiveness for stealing her husband. Sure he does, Anne thought wryly. They had been divorced a little over a year and still she felt the loss and cursed the day Philip walked into their lives.

Chapter Three

It took Natalie three days to find out that Hilton had slept with
another woman. Hilton was soaking in the bath in the big house
and listening to a tape of Anne's radio program on her portable
player. She had to resort to using the first-floor bathroom because
the third-floor tub was no longer useable. The white porcelain
handle had come off while she was rinsing out the tub so unless she
wanted a cold bath it was time to pick another bathroom. She was
thinking about the show. She'd be acting in the capacity of an offi-
cial observer all week. The Web site needed visuals. Hilton was
spoiled from listening to Anne and watching her. Having seen
Anne's facial expressions as she took calls and made commentary
would be priceless video footage. Her chair-spinning and paper-
tapping gave the conversations more pluck. It was difficult now
just to listen to the show.

Tomorrow she'd go in early and set up a Web cam to test out
her idea. If she could stream the program, the Web site would be a

new hotspot for her listeners and certainly fulfill all of Anne's expectations for redesigning her site.

Amid this revelry of how to please the new boss, Nat burst into the bathroom. Her face was flushed and Hilton could tell she was fit to be tied. She had a pretty good idea why. Word had obviously gotten out. Not that she was hiding the fact that she'd also spent most of Saturday night in the arms of another woman. She would have preferred, however, that it stay quiet. She hadn't seen Emily since then but it didn't mean she wouldn't in the future.

"What the fuck is going on?" Nat said, picking up the tape player and threatening to throw it in the bathtub.

"You won't get away with it. Remember that *Columbo* show where the son killed off his father by dunking the radio in the tub. Every cop in the world is aware of that stunt."

"Fuck you," Nat said. She clicked the player off and put it on the vanity. "You're sleeping with some baby dyke down the street."

"And?" Hilton said, slinking back down into the tub now that her life was no longer in jeopardy.

"And I'm pissed off." Nat put her hands on her slim hips. She was dressed in tight black hip-hugger jeans and a low-cut red T-shirt that prominently showed her cleavage.

"Is that like an authoritative pose?" Hilton said.

"Yes. What the hell do you think you're doing?"

"The same thing you're doing with the biker chick. I believe it's called retaliatory fucking."

"Great term. Did you learn that in therapy?"

Nat always reverted to therapy when she was at a loss on how to deal with Hilton. This was her way of reminding Hilton that she was not of sound mind and needed a nut ball like Nat to tell her how to behave in this savage world. Hilton had long stopped being offended. Therapy had been her father's idea because he was convinced that a six-year-old seeing her mother strewn out on the beach, seaweed in her hair, and drowned was a traumatic event. It had been a shocking sight, but it was anger, not trauma, that guided her into adulthood.

"I'm not sleeping with Sherry," Nat said with a sigh.

"What are you waiting for? That special moment? Or maybe you found someone with a conscience."

Nat's face flushed. "It's not that."

"Look, you started all this business. You're about to bang the biker chick and I'm doing the neighbor. What's the big deal?" Hilton kept her voice even and her face placid. Nat hated these self-contained moments. She wanted tears and platitudes. She wanted a scene. Hilton refused to indulge her. She wanted to make this as painful as possible. This was what the therapist would call passive-aggressive behavior.

"What's that supposed to mean?"

"It means maybe Sherry doesn't want to bang a married woman, maybe she's not comfortable doing someone else's woman, maybe she thinks monogamy is important and you haven't figured out a way to convince her that it's all right," Hilton retorted.

Nat swung open the bathroom door. "Fuck you!" she screamed.

Hilton had thrown the decisive blow. She was a marksman when it came to pinpointing a weak spot and hitting hard. "I can't. I probably don't have a big enough dildo to compete with the ever-hard biker chick."

Nat turned around and smiled. "As a matter of fact, you don't."

It was Hilton's turn to snap. She grabbed the soap and hurled it with the precision of a big-league pitcher. It nailed Nat in the back of the head.

"God damn you," Nat said, turning back around and going for Hilton. Liz and Jessie, who were watching reruns of *Leave it to Beaver* on television in the living room, heard the commotion and grabbed Nat before she got to the bathroom.

"I think a little time out might be in order," Liz said, putting her arm around Nat and leading her away.

Jessie stood in the doorway of the bathroom. "Great shot!"

Hilton rolled her eyes and got up and grabbed a towel. She dried off and put on her robe. Jessie looked on admiringly.

"You've got a great body," Jessie said, sitting down on the commode. She obviously meant to stay.

Hilton smiled. "The lucky sperm club is responsible for genetics, not character."

"What the hell does that mean?" Jessie asked. She picked up the fingernail clippers and decided her nails needed a little work.

This was more togetherness than Hilton preferred but it was going to have to do. Jessie looked parked. "It means what you look like is simply a happy accident, and how you behave is of your own making."

"I'd take happy accident any day. So I don't get it."

"Get what?" Hilton said, brushing her hair.

"Why you're in trouble when Nat is the one who plays."

"Go figure," Hilton said. She sat down on the edge of the slowly draining tub and applied lotion to her legs. She was going to have to employ a plumber, just not a lesbian plumber this time. Perhaps one afternoon when Nat was getting her brains fucked out she could bring someone in to repair the bathtubs at least. Maybe this time they'd get the pipes fixed instead of getting her girlfriend laid.

"I have a couple of theories," Jessie offered.

"In your ever-humble opinion on lesbian life."

"I have had a lot of experience when it comes to women."

"Oh, do share."

Jessie was never daunted by Hilton's facetiousness. This was a good quality, Hilton had deduced. Most people shut off when taunted. Jessie seemed to view it as kindling. It was going to be a roaring fire.

"It comes down to you get what you give."

"That's it?" Hilton wished she had more body maintenance to do because Jessie wasn't going to let her leave. She found her clothes and began dressing.

"Yes, you see there are basically three types of relationships."

"Only three?" Hilton pulled on her shorts and thought about running by the Army and Navy store downtown to pick up some camouflage pants. Fall was beginning to linger in the air. Her friend Doug at the store had told her a new shipment was due in any day. This was the first fall of her life when she wouldn't be going back to school, and she was finding a welcome relief in starting what might appear to be a new life. She had promised Gran she'd finish college and she'd fulfilled her promise.

"Yes, three—good, mediocre and bad. A good one is basically monogamous and long-term, or it's a roll in the hay that doesn't require the U-Haul at the end of the date. Then there's mediocre, two people who have the roll in the hay and feel obligated to turn a one-night stand into at least a two-year relationship. One or both partners want out but don't want the attached failure. Then there's bad, which describes you and Nat, two people who are together but shouldn't be." Jessie stopped her pontification, got up off the commode and set the nail clippers on the counter.

"That clears up everything for me."

"Glad I could help."

"Are you guarding me?" Hilton asked as it suddenly dawned on her that Jessie had an ulterior motive for keeping her contained.

"Yes, but it appears the coast is clear. Liz told me to keep you busy for at least five minutes until she got Nat safely escorted off the premises."

"I can always count on you two."

Liz showed up. "Well, at least you didn't put out an eye with that stunt." She put her hands on her hips with the obvious intention of getting some form of remorse out of Hilton.

"With a bar of soap?" Jessie asked.

Liz gave her the look. "Well, I mean, I guess you could, but it doesn't really seem all that plausible."

"Did she go running into the arms of the Dildo Queen?" Hilton asked snidely.

"I didn't ask," Liz replied. "Why don't you come watch the rest of *Leave It to Beaver* with us."

"Stupid show. Besides, I've got work to do," Hilton said. She made her way to the attic and tried to forget about Nat.

≈≈≈

Wednesday morning Hilton was at the radio station an hour and a half early. The show didn't start until ten. Shannon came in and did her perfunctory smell of the control room and then went out and lay down under the fan on the wooden floor of the office part of the studio. Hilton had deduced that Shannon found the control room too confined and noisy for her nap hour. She put her head down and closed her eyes. Inside Studio C she set up the Web cam and ran all the software so she could check the system before Anne went on the air. She double-checked the position of the camera. She walked by Studio B and waved at the new jock spinning tunes on the local FM station. It was his second day but he appeared to be doing just fine. Hilton liked him already because he was into social satire. Satisfied with her work she went to get a coffee. On the way out, Veronica, the show's producer, stopped her.

"Hilton, may I have a word with you?"

"Sure," Hilton said, thinking Veronica's requests were never that; they were standing orders. Hilton was doing her best but Veronica was not easy.

"It's about your wardrobe."

Just then Anne came around the corner. "What's wrong with her outfit?"

"I just think it should be more professional. I mean, a white men's undershirt in dire need of bleaching and camouflage cargo pants are hardly suitable business attire."

Hilton looked down at herself as if seeing her outfit for the first time. "No one sees me. It's radio."

"I just think when you get your first check you should go out and get yourself some nice clothes. I could figure in an advance if you'd like," Veronica offered. She ran her hand over her well-coiffed brunette bun.

"You're serious?" Anne said.

Hilton could see absolute mirth dancing in Anne's eyes because Hilton's secret of being an heiress was not information Veronica had been privy to as of yet.

"Have you known me to be anything else?" Veronica said.

"Uh, no." Anne took off her black blazer and put it around Hilton's shoulders. Hilton slipped her arms into it and then stood there feeling distinctly uncomfortable. The blazer smelled of Anne's perfume and it was still warm.

"Veronica, I think Hilton's basic philosophy on clothes is to pick something off the floor, give it a good sniff, determine whether it's inhabitable and then get dressed. Am I correct?"

Hilton nodded.

"But she has such nice lines," Veronica said, running her hand along Hilton's chin and checking her out.

Hilton shuddered.

"I think we're making her uncomfortable. Let's go," Anne said. She put her arm around Hilton's blazer-clad shoulders and led her to the control room. "Do you think Veronica's a lesbian? I can't quite figure her out."

"I hope not," Hilton said, horrified by the thought.

Anne laughed. "For your sake, me too. I think she might have the hots for you. She's already trying to cast you in her own image."

"If I ever show up in a bun and a tight black shirt with a herringbone blazer, shoot me because I've completely lost my mind."

"I promise. She is a great producer."

"She scares me."

Dave was sitting at the board doing show prep. He looked up. "Nice outfit."

"It's highbrow grunge," Anne said.

"Is there a dress code?" Hilton asked, genuinely concerned. No one had mentioned one and how did Anne know about her housekeeping methods? Were they that apparent?

"Hell, no!" Dave said. "Has Veronica been at you? She does that to all the new people. She has yet to make a convert. Just think of her as the Jehovah's Witness of fashion. She's always knocking but no one answers."

Anne laughed hysterically. Hilton was still puzzled. "My only stipulation is that you wear clothes. You look just like Dave except for the underwear."

Hilton blushed.

"Dare I ask? Let me venture . . . boxers?" Anne inquired, raising an eyebrow.

Hilton nodded. "They're much more comfortable."

"Really? I can't say I've tried them. You know, that would make a great show segment. The news is kind of slow today." Anne summoned Veronica to the control room. "Veronica, I need you to get me a pair of boxers immediately. I'm thinking a burgundy paisley would be nice, in silk, of course. What do you think?"

Veronica stood at the door looking perturbed. "I'm not a message boy."

"No, but you're a great shopper. Now get going, the show starts in forty-five minutes. I've got show prep to think of."

Veronica went stomping off and Hilton could tell she didn't like being treated as the office gofer. Serves her right for being a clothes Nazi, Hilton thought smugly.

"So what's this?" Anne asked, looking at the Web cam Hilton had set up.

"I want to videotape the show and run the stream on the Web site."

"Are you serious?"

"Yes, you'll need to put your blazer back on so you'll look presentable," Hilton said as she took it off and handed it to her.

"Right," Anne said, looking all business. She put the blazer on and straightened out the collar.

"Yeah, 'cause you know Veronica won't like it if you look sloppy," Dave said.

"I don't know if I'm entirely comfortable with this idea. What if I look bad on camera?"

"I've seen your promotion pictures. You're very photogenic. You'll look great. Besides, most listeners expect radio people to be homely. In this case, I think they'll be pleasantly surprised," Hilton said.

"Oh, well, since you put it that way," Anne said with a laugh.

Hilton smiled and led Anne to her chair in the booth. "Let's see how this works." She went into the control room and adjusted the frames, had Anne move around in her chair and then had Anne come back to the control room and look at the video stream on the computer.

"Hey, that actually works," Anne said, obviously pleased with Hilton's efforts.

"I am not late for work!" an elderly woman said emphatically as she marched across the room. Thick black-rimmed glasses magnified her pale blue eyes. She was wearing a purple flowered print dress and an enormous red hat with a long black feather. She nearly took out Hilton's eye as she stormed by in her beige square-heeled shoes. She seriously looked like she'd escaped from the old folks' home down the street.

"No, Lillian, I wasn't talking to you. I was saying it works," Anne enunciated, pointing to the Web cam.

"I always leave at the same time, take the same bus and arrive at the same time. Consequently, it's not possible that I'm late," Lillian said. She peered down at Shannon, who was sprawled out on the floor sound asleep.

"Yes, Lillian, I know," Anne said.

"And what on God's green earth is that?" Lillian said, nudging Shannon with her foot.

Shannon groaned.

"It's Hilton's dog, Shannon," Anne replied.

Shannon opened her eyes and then licked Lillian's ankle.

"I had a boyfriend that used to do that," Lillian said. She eased over gently and patted Shannon's head. "Nice doggy. I read an article the other day that pets in the workplace are supposed to reduce your blood pressure. Is she on the payroll?"

"Of course," Anne said.

"Pity she can't do promo work. We could replace you-know-who with the tight hair," Lillian said, nodding in Veronica's direction.

Anne laughed. "I'm going to go do some quick research on the history of underwear." She left for her booth.

Shannon followed her, having obviously decided that since everyone had filled their spaces in the control room that it was too crowded. She returned to her usual spot in center of the floor under the fan in the main office.

"Who is that?" Hilton whispered to Dave.

"She's the call screener."

"The call screener is deaf?" she asked incredulously.

"Yeah," he said, going back to setting up the board.

"But you've been screening calls all this week."

"Lillian was on vacation visiting her older sister in Phoenix," he said matter-of-factly.

"She has a sister older than her?"

"Yeah, and get this, they're both chain-smokers . . . Pall Mall Reds. So much for the healthy lifestyle crap."

"This doesn't make any sense."

"Welcome to monkey-land," Dave said.

"How can she screen calls if she can't hear the callers?"

"She can't. That's the beauty of it." He leaned over to check out Hilton's handiwork. "This is really going to improve ratings on the Web site."

"Thanks," Hilton said, trying not to blush.

Forty minutes later, Veronica breezed into the studio with a small bag from Nordstrom's and handed it to Anne who was sitting on the couch in the anterior of the studio reading her research notes on underwear. "Are you sure this is an appropriate topic for our listeners?" She raised her eyebrow and pursed her lips.

Hilton smirked, thinking someone like Anne Counterman didn't get where she was by listening to everything her producer told her. Hilton was getting the sense that Anne did what she wanted when and how she saw fit.

"I'm going to change. I'll be right back," Anne said, glancing up at the big clock on the back wall. In radio everyone lived by that clock. It was eight minutes to the top of the hour.

When she came back, Dave and Hilton were sitting on the

32

couch waiting for her. Lillian still had her head down on the control room desk taking a quick power nap. Dave had assured Hilton that this was an every day occurrence and that she'dbe pumped and ready to go when the show started. Anne walked around a bit, adjusted her black linen trousers and nodded. "These are more comfortable, not to mention that they totally alleviate the pantyline issue. Okay, we'll start the show off with the underwear discussion. Got that, Lillian?" Anne said, leaning into the control room door. Lillian woke with a start.

"Underwater? Like fish stories?" Lillian inquired, abruptly sitting straight up.

"No, like boxers," Anne said.

"I knew a boxer once. He had terrible table manners," Lillian said.

"Just remember, anything to do with clothes is fine," Anne suggested. She gave Dave a pregnant look.

"I'll watch her," Dave muttered.

The intro music for the show started. Anne's theme song for the show was Aretha Franklin's song, "Respect." Hilton took her seat in the control room and watched the video stream on the ancillary monitor she'd set up. This was going to work awesome.

Anne did an impromptu monologue on the virtues of underwear from the research she'd done on the Internet. She gave a brief history and then extolled the virtues of various undergarments. Dave switched on the top-of-the-hour news and weather along with station identification for KCOM-FM while Lillian screened calls. Hilton carefully monitored the video stream.

"There's someone here who wants to talk about thongs," Lillian screamed. "Is beachwear what we've sunk to?"

Dave reached over and transferred the call. Anne gave him the thumbs-up signal.

"It's a slow news day, Lillian," Anne said.

"Hello, Anne, this is Heather and I am wearing a thong."

"Aren't they uncomfortable?" Anne asked.

"No, not at all. They make you feel free, not stifled by excess fabric," the breathy voice said.

"Are you a leggy blonde?" Anne inquired. She rolled her eyes and smiled mischievously at the video cam.

"Of course. You must be psychic," the woman said.

"You've got heels on right now, don't you?"

The woman laughed flirtatiously.

Satisfied with the video stream, Hilton went to get a bottle of water from the employee lounge that was located just down the hall from the studio. She noticed the FedEx driver standing at the reception area obviously waiting for the receptionist's return.

"Hey, can I get you to sign for something," the driver said.

"Am I allowed to do that?" Hilton asked.

"Sure, I just need a signature. It's a package for Hilton Withers. Does she work here?"

"Oh, that's me. I can sign for my own package, right?"

"Boy, she's got you freaked already," the driver said.

Hilton smirked apologetically for having no balls. She couldn't think of anything she'd ordered. Still puzzled, she signed for the package. The FedEx driver was a short, buff, Hispanic woman who stared intently at her while she signed the form. Hilton looked up and smiled politely.

"You must be new," the driver said.

"Yes, I'm Hilton," she said, extending her hand. She refused to be snotty. She had done that once to a homely girl in her class when she was growing up and Gran had berated her for her unkindness and belligerence, for thinking herself better because she was lucky enough to be born pretty. Hilton had never forgotten that discussion. Unfortunately, being polite sometimes gave the impression she was interested. It was a difficult balance.

"I'm Dolores. Nice to meet you, Hilton. Do you order a lot of stuff?"

"Yes, computer stuff mostly. I'm kind of a tech geek."

"You look pretty hip for a geek," Dolores said.

Hilton wondered if this was a potential come-on. She smiled anyway. She could always pull her famous "I've got a lot on my plate right now" response if need be. It usually worked.

The break came and Anne signed off while the commercials set in. She was on her way to the break room to get a cup of coffee. Hilton watched as Anne arched her eyebrow as she passed by.

"So haven't I seen you . . . out," Dolores said.

The emphasis on the word *out* was code for gay bar. Hilton laughed. "Perhaps a time or two," she replied coyly.

"I thought so," Dolores said with a knowing smile.

Veronica came swishing by the reception desk. "Don't you have packages to deliver?" she said curtly.

Dolores just smiled conspiratorially and leaned closer to Hilton. "Don't touch that one."

"Oh, no . . . really."

"Grave mistake," Dolores said.

"Girlfriend, what were you thinking?"

"What can I say? Momentary lapse of judgment. I'll see you around, Hilton."

" 'Bye, Dolores." Hilton made sure she said it loud enough for Veronica to hear. She knew they could be friends now because Hilton had treated her as a fellow hunter and not game. Besides, it appeared being nice to Dolores really pissed off Veronica so that made it all the better.

Hilton took the package back to the studio and sat on the leather couch in the anterior. The commercials were playing. There was still station identification and thirty seconds of bumper music to get through. She opened the package to find the largest dildo she'd ever laid eyes on. It was dark purple. She pulled it out of the box and eyed it ominously.

"What the hell is that?" Dave asked, peeking out from the control room.

"It's a dog toy," Hilton said. She threw it to Shannon, who was still lying on the floor of the anterior underneath the huge brass ceiling fan. Luckily, Lillian was out having a cigarette.

"It looks more like a . . ." Dave said, wincing as Shannon chewed on the end of it.

"A penis?" Hilton said, finishing his sentence because he didn't seem capable.

"Well, yeah."

"It's commonly referred to as a dildo." Hilton took her seat in the control room.

"I didn't realize they came that large," Dave said, watching Shannon acutely.

"What d'ya mean? I thought all you guys were hung like horses," Hilton teased.

"Not like that!" Dave replied. "That's obscene."

Hilton laughed.

"Who sent that?"

"My girlfriend," Hilton said. "It's a retort for a discussion we had that ended with me nailing her in the back of the head with a bar of soap."

"Lemme guess, she caught you in the bath where you were held captive. Why do women do that?"

"Because we're evil," Hilton replied, thinking Nat must have headed straight to FedEx the evening before. She watched as Anne came back from the bathroom, still adjusting her pants.

"You've got to kind of tuck them down in your pants," she noted. She bent down to scratch Shannon's ears.

Hilton and Dave sat quiet as she looked at Shannon's new chew toy.

Her face grew puzzled. "I didn't realize chew toys came in that particular configuration," she said, cocking her head to one side to get a better look.

"It's new," Dave said.

Lillian came back from her cigarette break just as Anne entered the booth. "What the hell is that! It looks like a giant penis."

Both Dave and Hilton burst out laughing, and Dave nearly fell out of his chair.

Anne sat down in her booth and must have noticed the ruckus on the other side of the glass. She got up and looked at the dog toy again. "Is that what I think it is?" she said into the mike.

Dave was gasping and couldn't respond.

"It's a present from Natalie."

"Do I want to know any more?" Anne asked.

36

"Probably not," Hilton replied.

The bumper music stopped and the show began. Anne took another call about the virtues of briefs versus boxers. "So let me get this straight, the package is more prominent in briefs than boxers?"

"Absolutely," a flamboyant male voice said. "I mean, one should make the most of one's, shall we say, accoutrements."

"Gotcha," Anne replied.

Dave was waving wildly at Hilton who was now in the anterior room with Shannon. Anne was still talking to the fag and gave Dave the "what's up?" signal. Dave beeped in on her ISB, which allowed him to "talk in her ear" without the audience hearing. "Tour group."

Anne mouthed, "So?"

Dave pointed to Hilton, who was frantically attempting to retrieve the giant dildo from Shannon, who was having none of it. The dildo was hers and she wasn't giving it up without a fight. Hilton had one end of it and Shannon was pulling fiercely on the other end.

"Thank you, caller, for your insights and now we've got some office business going on. Listeners, I believe I've been remiss in telling you about the new addition to our staff."

Hilton stopped pulling for a moment and looked up at Anne, who waved.

"Her name is Hilton and she's our new Webmistress. She's a lesbian. I can tell you that because the entire Senate and I'm sure the House of Representatives and even our fair-haired son of a president has been informed of Hilton's sexual orientation. I say orientation because I think preference is like I prefer cream in my coffee or I prefer French fries instead of mashed potatoes. One does not prefer to be a social pariah. One does not prefer to be ostracized, prefer to be an abomination, prefer to be cut off from one's family, live outside of the law, face discrimination, worry about being a victim of hate crimes, et cetera! Oh, and all you people who are going to call in and tell me that all the homos should be shipped off to Homoslavia, don't bother, heard it all before. Lillian, our call screener, is a big old dyke who could kick your ass any day of the week. So homophobes need not apply here."

"If I've told you once I've told you a thousand times I take the bus to work. I do not ride a bike," Lillian screamed.

Hilton stopped what she was doing for a moment and asked Dave, "Why does she scream?" She and Shannon had inched closer to the control room and were still playing tug-of-war just outside the open door.

"I don't know, maybe because she can't hear, she thinks the rest of us can't either," he said, shrugging.

Hilton went back to wrestling with Shannon in a last-ditch attempt to gain control of the object of desire before the tour group made it down the hall. Anne didn't seem too awfully concerned about the situation. Rather, she continued narrating the scene for her listeners.

"Hilton is a whiz kid with the computer and a looker for the ladies. I mean, she's hot, and I say that from a straight woman's perspective. Dave, our broadcast engineer, is going to lose one of his hands if he keeps sticking it in his mouth and biting it every time Hilton goes by. Don't you dare," Anne said, indicating that Dave was going to bleep that part out. "No editing is allowed. This is a freestyle show."

Hilton let the remark pass unnoticed to let Dave save face. Besides, she was still busy attempting to extricate the dildo from Shannon.

"Now, where was I before we were rudely interrupted by the broadcast engineer's attempt at censorship. Anyway, Hilton is doing her best to extricate a giant purple dildo from her dog Shannon's ferocious pearly whites. I mean, this dog is not going to let go. Shannon, for you dog-lovers out there, is a white Pyrenees that I'm thinking weighs at least a hundred pounds. Hilton might weigh a hundred pounds dripping wet. So who do you think is winning? My odds are on the dog. The aforementioned purple object—I don't know how many times I can say dildo on the air

38

and not have the FCC threatening to rip out my vocal cords. So from now on the dildo—there, I did it again, somebody slap me—will be referred to as the aforementioned purple object. It was a present from Hilton's girlfriend and I'm thinking it's either a practical joke, a not very good one, or some kind of a sexual slur. I know this is because I'm a woman and women, in general, are vicious. I'm thinking we could exclude Mother Teresa and Betty White. That woman can't have a mean bone in her body, even if she is Hollywood folk. She would bake Michael Moore some cookies, I'm thinking four dozen, maybe more if he asked her. Anyway, it appears Hilton made the mistake of regifting the object to Shannon. Right now, I'm thinking Hilton would prefer to be anywhere but here. Hey, Hilton, didn't anyone tell you possession is nine-tenths of the law? Oh, listeners, it gets better. The tour group headed up by our prim and proper producer, Veronica, is now coming by. This bunch of radio buffs are about to be treated to quite a sight. Now, for those of you who have never been to a radio station, let me describe it for you. We have the soundproof booth that I'm in and then we have the outside studio that houses the control room where the broadcast engineer and the call screener sit, and then there is a big picture window at the back of the studio that allows the rest of the world to spy on us. Oh, yes, here we go. Hilton has almost won the tug-of-war. The group has stopped. Some of the older women are looking at the aforementioned item with a mixture of awe and wonder. Perhaps they're thinking that their husbands are not so well-endowed after all. That six-inch rule is coming to fruition, gentlemen."

Hilton saw Anne stand up and wave genially to her audience. Hilton was still tugging when Shannon obviously lost concentration and let go of the desired object. Unfortunately, Hilton was unaware of this new development. She ended up flat on her back holding the dildo straight up in the air. Anne quickly signaled for a break because she was laughing so hard she couldn't speak. Dave's face was so red he looked like he might need oxygen. Lillian sighed in disgust as she stepped over Hilton and went outside to have another cigarette. Hilton could have rolled over and died.

Anne took the dildo from her, dog slime and all, and studied it. "My God! This is impressive. Hilton, you've done something I've never been able to do."

Hilton sat up. "What's that?"

"Embarrass Veronica to the very core of her being."

Dave started to breath again. "Not to mention I've got it all on video."

"How the hell did you do that?" Hilton asked.

"I disconnected the cam to Anne's booth and plugged in the extra one you'd brought. It was really quite simple. Sorry, boss, but I had to make an executive decision and what was happening here was obviously more important."

"Good call. Remind me to put you both in for a Christmas bonus."

"I can't wait for the Christmas party," Dave said, quickly going back to the control room. He checked the board and put on the bottom-of-the-hour news and weather.

Anne, Hilton and Dave were lounging in the studio on the couch after the show when Ed walked into the room. All antics stopped and Shannon did what Hilton wished she could do—creep into the control room and crawl under the nearest desk. Hilton mouthed the word "coward." Shannon just whimpered. Hilton figured this was the end of her radio career.

Ed stood in the middle of the room while the suspense built. His stern face erupted into a smile. He started clapping. "Good show. The only casualty was Veronica getting her knickers in a twist, and I suspect they're always a little askew, but we got good feedback. Veronica is insisting that I put out a memo that forbids certain paraphernalia on the studio floor."

"I can live with that," Anne said.

Hilton and Dave nodded in unison. Ed winked at them. He left, shutting the door behind him.

They all broke down into fits of laughter.

"Let me see that thing," Anne said.

"You try getting it away from Shannon," Hilton said. She sat down and took a deep breath.

Later that afternoon, Hilton sat on the steps of the back porch. She liked her new schedule. She basically worked from eight-thirty to two, depending on how well the Web site update went. She was alone in the house for once. Liz and Jessie were still in class and Nat was nowhere to be found. The flower gardens had long gone to seed except for the hardy vincas, which ended up being tall on stem and short on flowers. Still, their shiny dark green leaves gave some color to the vast array of browns and yellows. The Chinese dogwood trees that lined the back fence had littered the lawn with burgundy leaves. Fall was in the air and for the first time in her life Hilton felt grownup. She didn't know exactly what it was or how it came to be. But she felt sort of responsible.

Maybe the evil bitch Veronica was right about dressing for success. Maybe it was time to change her femi-nazi attire and give the business world a try. She wasn't a college kid anymore. Although she wasn't entirely sure what she wanted to do with the rest of her life, maybe it was time to leave off parties, getting laid and generally shirking responsibility. She wondered if her extended childhood may have had something to do with Gran dying. If the old woman had still been alive, the house shenanigans would never have evolved to their current state and Hilton would have been expected to have a grownup career by now.

She looked over at Shannon, who was unmercifully chewing off the head of the dildo. Hilton inwardly flinched as she relived the day's episode. Thank God Anne had a sense of humor.

"What's up?" Liz asked as she came around the corner lugging a giant book bag.

"Boy, I don't miss that," Hilton said, pointing to the knapsack.

"I'll say. Why the hell are textbooks so, I don't know, substantial? I swear they're trying to kill us off before we have a chance to graduate." She plopped down next to Hilton on the porch steps.

"They are. The professors want to make sure they don't have any up-and-coming competition."

"With tenure they have no worries. My God, when will the old farts retire?"

"How's your new job at the computer lab?"

"It's pretty good. I'm basically being paid to baby-sit. I have to make sure everyone has a spill-proof cup and that no one carts off a computer." Liz pointed at Shannon's new toy. "What is that?"

"It's a dildo that's approximately ten minutes from the trash can."

Shannon barked in protest and put a protective paw over it.

"She has a larger vocabulary than some of my peers."

"I think you're forgetting who's the alpha dog here." Hilton pointed a finger at Shannon, who appeared to make a point of ignoring her.

"Why is she chewing on a dildo?"

Hilton relayed the story, which left Liz sputtering and wiping her eyes on her shirt sleeve.

"Can I see the video?"

"No!" Hilton said.

"How about if I make my famous lasagna, garlic bread and a tossed salad with red vinegar and oil dressing with fresh parmesan—and a nice bottle of Merlot."

Hilton groaned. "You know I'm a complete whore for good food." It was almost five-thirty and she hadn't had any lunch.

"Video?"

"After dinner."

"Deal. Oh, I can hardly wait. I better get started," Liz said, getting up quickly.

They heard the rumble of the Harley as it pulled up in the driveway.

"I hope she's wearing a helmet," Liz said.

"She better be because I'm not wiping her ass when she's a paraplegic."

"Hilton!"

"Hey," Nat said as she came around the corner of the house.

"Tell me you wear a helmet when you're on that bike," Liz demanded.

"Sherry makes me." Nat sat on the grass next to Shannon and scratched her ears.

Hilton glared at Shannon, who appeared not to notice. It was if she were saying, "You may be mad at her but I'm not."

"How chivalrous." Hilton sniffed.

"Is that—?" Nat said, noticing the badly mangled dildo.

"Yes, as a matter of fact it is. Shannon adores it."

Hilton watched as Liz's face grew tense. It didn't seem to bother Nat in the least.

"Now, that must have been a sight walking down the street." Nat picked up the dildo, examined it and then gave it back to Shannon.

"Better yet, at the office. It's grotesque."

"Wait until you see the video of them—Hilton, Shannon, the dildo and the tour group," Liz said. Hilton gave her a look, to which she responded, "It's probably all over the Internet by now."

"It's not," Hilton said emphatically.

"Video of them doing what?" Nat asked.

"Never mind," Hilton said.

Nat pouted. "You're still mad at me? I was the one who got nailed with the soap. I still have a bump on the back of my head." She rubbed the spot for emphasis.

"If I remember correctly you tried to electrocute me." Hilton twitched and quivered for effect.

"You didn't tell me that!" Liz said, giving Nat an accusatory glance as she leaned against the worn railings of the small porch.

"Oh, did I forget to mention that?" Nat said coyly.

"You did."

"Come on, can't we get past that?" Nat got up off the grass and sat next to Hilton on the porch.

"You slept with her," Hilton said.

Nat smiled. "Now we're even, aren't we?"

"I'll go start dinner," Liz said. She closed the screen door quietly behind her.

Hilton didn't say anything. Nat took her hand. "Why do we have to be like this?"

"Because you have a phobia about commitment."

"I do not!"

"Then why do you date other people?"

Nat appeared to be thinking. Hilton waited.

"Because I can," Nat ventured.

Hilton sighed. "That's lame. Try again."

"Because I love you too much to lose you, but monogamy isn't good for a relationship. Because my parents have such a hideous relationship that it frightens me. Because I have an inadequate sense of self—"

Hilton cut her short. "Oh, please, you probably have a little black book filled with these lines. They're out of some psychology class you took in your first year of college."

"They are not. I'm sorry I made such a stink about your latest liaison. I was totally out of line."

"Great."

"What?" Nat pulled out a cigarette from her knapsack.

"I just want us to have a normal relationship."

Nat lit her cigarette and laughed. "Listen, normal equates to misery. Look at our friends. At best they tolerate each other. What we've got is a lot better. I should never have said anything about the neighbor. I broke our cardinal rule, and for that I prostrate myself and beg your forgiveness."

"Please," Hilton said. She studied Nat as she smoked her cigarette. It dawned on her that Nat had no sense of danger, of consequence, of anything beyond today. Tomorrow didn't matter and when it did she'd worry about it then. It was sort of like some polluted, warped kind of Zen. All that mattered was this moment and perhaps the next five minutes. The rest was irrelevant. What was past was finished. What was future was too mercurial to worry about. Hilton took Nat's hand. "Maybe you'll love me totally when you're old and wrinkly and no one else wants you." She could smell the pasta cooking and the pungent smell of spaghetti sauce.

Nat laughed. "You know I probably will. Now, let's go check on dinner."

They ambled inside. Liz looked down at their joined hands and Hilton could sense her relief. All was right with the family again. For now, Hilton thought.

Chapter Four

Anne was looking at the Web site Hilton had created. The past two weeks had been a blur and here it was Friday night and she still couldn't get enough. Her mother was correct. She was a workaholic, but one didn't get to the top of the radio talk scene without wholehearted dedication coupled with complete obsession. According to her mother, Victoria Anne Counterman, this was why her husband, Gerald, had left her. Anne pissed on her mother's opinions once again. The Web site traffic was growing steadily. This meant a new market for sponsors and if the traffic continued it would increase revenue as more advertisers became interested, so Victoria-mother-of-all knowing-mothers could just go fuck herself, Anne thought smugly.

"I'm going to be happily obsessed," Anne said to the empty room.

Perhaps the part Anne found most satisfying about the last two weeks was that she was interested in the show again. It was difficult admitting to herself that at thirty-nine her lifelong dream bored her. The worst part for someone who shared her life with the world was that she had to keep this a secret. How could she tell her loyal followers or her devoted staff that some days she was bored to distraction, that she could care less about the day's topic or the caller's opinion. She, Anne Counterman, hated her job. It was a disgrace to herself and she was perpetrating a fraud on her listeners. This had been plaguing her daily until Hilton had walked into her life, and all of a sudden the show became fun again. It's a good God damn thing, Anne thought, leaning back in her black leather chair. Hilton, of course, had no idea this was occurring, but that was of little consequence. It was better to be a muse and not know it. Being an inspiration put pressure on a person and could inhibit their future productivity. She had often wondered if she'd done that to Gerald. Had she picked his brain too often? Had she sucked him dry emotionally with her need for approval and security? Had she sent him in search of calm, clear waters?

She exhaled loudly and shut her conscience off. What was done was done. She turned back to the Web site and began scrutinizing its parts. Speaking of creativity, she thought, the site should really have a message board where listeners could post notes to her as well as each other, a sort of online, off-air dialogue. That could spark tangents, and tangents were her forte. It could be a gold mine for brain-picking and she wouldn't have to risk a relationship in the process. "It's win-win," she said aloud.

She headed for the technical back end of the Web site. It shouldn't be that hard. She'd seen Hilton mucking around in it to change things. Surely, there would be a little icon or something for adding a message board. A box popped up indicating a password or the option to bypass. Anne thought nothing of it and opted for the bypass. She clicked the box and a message popped up on the screen. It read, "You have entered an unauthorized area. The system will now terminate itself." A set of symbols started running through all the screens like the program was eating its own tail.

"What the hell?" Anne said. "It was a trick."

It took about two minutes before it occurred to Anne what was happening. Hilton must have installed a virus so that if the program was violated in any way it would destroy itself.

"Oh, this is fucking great!" Anne frantically dialed Hilton's cell phone. Hilton had made mention that she lived in the university district but what was she to do, drive around the college until she found a pea-green Bug parked out front? In desperation she called Veronica and after much discussion and threatening her within an inch of her life, Veronica gave her Hilton's address.

Anne drove fast and redialed Hilton's cell phone a zillion times. In ten minutes she was in front of the Victorian house. The front yard was a parking lot and loud music emanated from the living room. It seemed every light was on in the house and the front door was wide open. Not knowing what else to do, Anne slipped inside with the rest of the party-goers.

She frantically looked around for Hilton. There must have been fifty people crammed into the living room and spilling down the hallway. She was about to ask the next passerby when a young woman with long dark hair grabbed her by the arm.

"What are you doing here?" the young woman asked her.

"Excuse me?" Anne said, slightly taken aback by the young woman's tone of voice.

"You're Anne Counterman, aren't you? You look just like your billboard."

"Yes. Look, I need to talk to Hilton. I did something to the Web site and it's all messed up. Can you help me find her?"

"You didn't bypass the password?" the woman asked. Her eyes got big.

Anne nodded.

"You're in big trouble. I'm Liz, by the way, one of Hilton's roommates."

"It's nice to meet you," Anne said, holding out her hand. Liz shook it firmly and Anne felt better immediately. This woman appeared competent.

Liz grabbed her shoulders and spun her around in an obvious

attempt to prevent her from seeing a topless woman in a g-string and red heels go marching by with a silver tray of Jell-O shots.

"Can I have one of those?" Anne asked the woman.

"Sure," a man's voice responded.

Anne watched as Liz cringed. She slugged down her shot and took a deep breath. "She's in transition, I take it," Anne said.

"Yes, Lyle is almost Lynette except for the last little snip. Let me take you upstairs, and try not to look at anything . . . please."

"I've seen things . . ." Anne started to say when another topless woman dressed in black Levis went by. Her nipples were pierced and two long chains connected them to rings above her eyebrows. "Okay, I haven't seen that before," she said stoically.

On the way upstairs Liz's efforts to avoid the wildness proved futile. Anne was offered a mirror with several lines of cocaine on it, got propositioned and on the second floor, was handed a joint that Liz quickly snatched and handed back to its owner. Once on the third floor, they turned left and climbed a small narrow set of stairs which ended at a door. Liz opened the door to the attic.

Anne took it in. The attic ran the length of the house with a high vaulted ceiling. It had finished walls and a wood floor. There was an old cloth couch on one wall and piles of records and tapes along with clothes strewn everywhere. At one end of the room was a stereo system shoved into what had once been bookcases. Anne thought the room must have been someone's hideaway. Next to the bookcases was an enormous desk that had a variety of computer equipment, some in pieces, others in perhaps working order. It looked like a mad scientist lived up there. The rest of the large room was filled with something that looked like a kidney-shaped swimming pool made out of wood. She could hear something scraping around in it. It was about four feet high on one end and almost six feet on the other. It reminded Anne of a large-scale architectural model and she couldn't for the life of her figure out what the hell it was.

"Hilton?" Liz called out.

Lyle Lovett was blaring on the stereo and Hilton's head and

body came flying up on the edge of the pool-like thing on a skate-board.

"Hilton," Liz screamed again.

Hilton popped up on the other side. "I didn't do it." Seconds later she came up on the other side. "I don't know where it is."

Another swoop and she said, "And yes, I am busy."

"Hilton, it's Anne. I think I destroyed the Web site."

"Anne?" Hilton seemed momentarily suspended in the air. She dropped the skateboard and disappeared into the bottom of the wooden structure. There was a loud crash. The skateboard resumed its course up the other side with so much force that it flew into the rafters and stuck there.

"Hilton, are you all right?" Anne asked.

Hilton groaned.

Anne was about to go see when Liz grabbed her arm. "Wait, put this on," she said and handed her a silver hard hat.

"What for?"

Liz pointed to the rafters, which were filled with an assortment of errant skateboards.

"Got it," Anne said. She put the hard hat on. It appeared that if one fell in this strange contraption you might send the skateboard into the attic rafters never to been seen again.

Liz and Anne climbed a short set of wooden stairs that led to a small deck where they could see Hilton lying flat on her back in the middle of the wooden structure.

"Are you all right?" Liz asked.

"Yeah, I just got the wind knocked out of me. Damn, I liked that skateboard," Hilton said, looking up at the ceiling.

"It'll come back down eventually," Liz said diplomatically.

"What is this thing, exactly?" Anne asked.

"It's a skate bowl. You enter from up here and you can ride the edges of the bowl. They used to do it all the time in California but they used drained swimming pools. Hilton had this one built along those same principles," Liz said.

"Oh, shit! Watch out." Hilton jumped to her feet and turned

50

her gaze to the rafters. The impact of the skateboard hitting the rafters must have loosened the other errant boards and four skateboards came careening down.

"You see, you lost one and gained four," Liz said.

Hilton surveyed her riches. "You're right. I really liked this one," she said, studying the design on the bottom. It was a flying dinosaur swooping over a primordial jungle.

Anne watched and waited for what she'd said to sink in.

"Did you say something about the Web site?"

"I wanted to put in a message board and so I bypassed the password."

"Did the message pop up mentioning termination of the program?"

"Uh, yes. That's not a very nice trick," Anne said.

"How long ago?"

"About twenty minutes."

Hilton took off her helmet and appeared lost in thought for a moment. She was wearing only boxer shorts and a sports bra. Hilton had a teenage boy's body, Anne thought, only with breasts. Her arms and back had visible muscle tone as did her torso and thighs.

"Okay, let me get dressed and we'll sort this out." She started rummaging around for clothes in the sundry piles littering the room. She looked at Shannon. "Well, which pile is clean or cleaner?"

It appeared to Anne that Hilton came up here to relax and just took off whatever she was wearing, which was why she had no clue as to its condition.

Shannon sniffed both piles and then barked, indicating which pile was clean. Hilton plucked off a T-shirt and a pair of black jeans. She got dressed quickly. Anne noticed that Hilton studiously avoided her gaze. Either she was embarrassed about her lack of clothing or her laundry situation.

"Come on," Hilton said.

"What are we going to do?"

"Find my Palm Pilot, which I'm hoping is in the bathroom with my knapsack. It has all my codes to get the computer to stop the termination. I have a timer set within the termination program, which gives us a little time, but the process has already started. I built in periods of rest so the person who violated the program has the option for negotiation."

Liz and Shannon followed them out of the room. "I think I'll go downstairs and try and tidy up a bit," Liz said.

"Great idea. Maybe Jessie can help," Hilton replied.

Anne saw the look that Hilton gave her. Anne smiled, thinking it was too late. She'd already seen most of what was out there. She'd had wild moments in her life. Being thirty-nine, shortly to be forty, did not automatically make one stodgy.

"I don't know. She seems to have gone missing with the committee chairwoman of Queer Nation. Something about flyers," Liz said as she scuttled down the stairs.

Anne followed Hilton to the bathroom.

"There you are," Hilton said. She stepped over a young woman's half-naked body that lay nestled between the legs of another woman. Hilton grabbed her knapsack, rustled around inside it and pulled out her Palm Pilot. She kissed it. "Thank God." She began scrolling through her programs looking for the codes.

"Hilton?"

"Yes," Hilton said, obviously distracted.

"There are people fornicating in your bathroom."

Hilton looked at the woman and her playmate. "Oh, shit!" She grabbed Anne's arm and whipped her around. "Jessie, couldn't you have picked a better spot?"

Jessie looked up from kissing the woman's torso. "Sorry. We just got caught up in the moment."

Hilton sighed heavily. "I found the codes. I had to put them in my address book using a series of fake phone numbers that when properly deciphered comprise the sequence necessary to stop the program and start the restoration process."

Anne took a deep breath. "I promise never to touch it again."

"You're forgiven. Now, let's go and see if we can fix it." Hilton led Anne downstairs. Her cell phone rang. She answered it on the third ring. "What did you say?" she screamed over the music. They entered the kitchen. Liz and Hilton stood looking at each other while holding their cell phones.

"I said don't bring her down here. Belinda is doing her circus tricks again."

All three of them turned around to see Belinda, a woman with the largest breasts Anne had ever seen, giving out whipped cream and white Russian shots. Anne watched as she sprayed her breasts with Redi-Whip and then wedged a shot glass between her breasts. A young woman with dyed pink hair dove into her cleavage and took the shot of liquor. The woman turned around to address the admiring crowd and spied Hilton.

"Hilton, they told me you were busy." She grabbed Hilton by the waist and pulled her close. She kissed her deeply, smearing whipped cream over both their faces.

"Does she have to do that in front of me," someone else screeched from the corner of the room.

Belinda gave Shannon a fingerful of whipped cream.

"No junk food. I told you about that," Hilton said, grabbing Shannon's collar.

"Like you have any room to talk," the pink-haired woman said, obviously taunting the other woman.

The other woman moved dangerously close. Liz stepped in between them. "Nat, that's enough. Let it go." Liz said to the petite brunette who was threatening the pink-haired woman. "Hilton, why don't you two leave and I'll take care of this."

They got to the car without further incident. Shannon hopped in the backseat of Anne's Chevy Avalanche.

"She loves your car."

Anne plucked a Kleenex out of the console. "Come here, you've got whipped cream everywhere." Their eyes met. "Hilton, is your house always like that?"

Clearly uncomfortable, Hilton smiled. "No, not at all."

"Oh, good."

"Usually, it's worse."

Anne stared at her. This was more than she had even ventured to imagine. She knew that Hilton was gay, that she was rich, that she was smart and that she might still be sowing some wild oats, but tonight was definitely an eye-opener. Anne did feel downright stodgy. Sometimes real life was stranger than fiction. Tonight seemed like something out of William Burrough's *Naked Lunch*.

"I'm kidding, kind of." She went back to fiddling with her Palm Pilot.

Anne started the car and drove toward the office. "Hilton?"

"Yes."

"So was the woman who kissed you your girlfriend?"

"Not exactly. The short brunette who wanted to kick her ass was my girlfriend, Natalie."

"Then who was the pink-haired woman who kissed you?" Anne figured that since Hilton was in an answering mood now was the time to get it all out. She had been curious about Hilton's life because as a student of human behavior, people interested her. This evening, however, had exceeded her wildest suppositions about her young intern's life.

"That was Emily. We had, shall we say, a liaison not long ago."

"Suffice it to say, Natalie isn't happy about it."

"No, but she's sleeping with some biker chick so she hardly has room to talk."

They were waiting at the stoplight. Anne could see Hilton's jaw tighten at the mention of this. "Oh, is this how most alternative relationships are conducted?" she asked.

"No."

Anne inwardly sighed with relief. For as much as she disliked her ex-husband's relationship with another man, she didn't want it going down the drain and Gerald out fucking someone else. Somehow their monogamous relationship made Anne feel better and somewhat justified in his leaving. If he had done it just for a quick fuck, she would have been really angry and feeling more inadequate than she already did. She was going to have to get over it someday. She just didn't know how.

"It's just that way with Nat and me."

"So what are you going to do about it?"

"Do?" Hilton repeated.

Anne pulled into the parking lot. "You know . . . about Natalie and Emily."

"Hope they both go away," Hilton said. "I'm beginning to think relationships are overrated. You seem pretty happy and stress-free."

"Except when I mess up Web sites." Anne parked the car. They went inside the building and got in the elevator. Shannon's tail was wagging and it kept making thumping noises against the stainless steel wall of the elevator.

"She loves to come to work."

"Even late at night. I am so sorry about this."

"It's all right. I'll fix it. Besides, it's only ten-thirty. She'll just nap until we're done. Won't you, girl?" Hilton said, reaching down to scratch her ears.

"I'll buy you breakfast."

"Deal." Hilton sat down at her computer in the empty control room and surveyed the damage.

Anne sat in Dave's chair and looked worried. Shannon lay down at Anne's feet and promptly fell asleep. "I hope in my next life I'm reincarnated as woman's best friend."

Hilton smiled and began typing.

Chapter Five

It was two o'clock in the morning by the time Hilton had completely repaired the Web site. The graveyard D.J. in the next studio waved as he walked past with a cup of coffee. Anne had worked out two complete opening monologues for the show. They looked at each other with bleary eyes.

"Okay, that was fun," Anne said facetiously. She straightened up her notes. She tried to crack her neck, which felt permanently cricked. Actually, the night had been rather pleasant as they chatted about Anne's ideas for the show and Hilton gave Anne a quick lesson on computer programming. Most of it was way over her head, but Anne enjoyed seeing Hilton thoroughly enthused about something. Anne realized she missed the closeness of having someone to exchange ideas with. It was times like these that she missed Gerald. They had spent evenings in like fashion.

"I think we'll pass on breakfast," Hilton said, rubbing her eyes. She got up and stretched.

Shannon barked in apparent protest.

"The McDonald's drive-through closed at one-thirty, as if I needed to remind you."

Shannon slumped down and let out a heavy sigh.

"I'm sure we can go out to breakfast with Anne some other time," Hilton told Shannon.

"We will. I swear," Anne said, holding up her three fingers in a Girl Scout pledge.

Shannon turned her head away.

"That was rude. Now, you go and apologize," Hilton reprimanded.

Shannon looked guilty. She got up and licked Anne's hand.

"That's better."

"Come on, let's get you two home," Anne said, searching for her car keys.

Hilton picked them up from beside the computer. "I'm going to get you one those electronic key finders for Christmas."

"What a lovely idea," Anne said. She slipped her car keys in her blazer pocket.

They left the building and woke up the security guard on the way out. He had been noticeably absent on their way in, Anne noted. She made a mental note to mention this fact to Veronica, who would look into the habits of the security guard with the tenacity of the former KGB.

"Did you want anything?"

"You mean to steal?" Hilton asked, apparently taken aback.

"Yes."

"Well, maybe something of Veronica's." Hilton smiled mischievously.

"Hilton!" Anne said. She opened the big glass doors of the building. The street lamps shone dimly, making white circles over the courtyard.

"She hurt my feelings with her comments on my attire. I actually started to question myself."

Anne put her arm around Hilton's shoulders. "Don't give her a second thought. You're perfect just the way you are."

Hilton blushed. "Thanks."

Shannon jumped in the backseat and sighed contentedly.

"I'm not getting you a Hummer," Hilton told her.

"How do you know she wants a Hummer?" Anne asked as she got in the driver's seat. She had yet to figure out the language that Hilton and Shannon used but they appeared to communicate better than most people did.

"Every time we walk past one or sit in traffic next to one, she gazes at it longingly and then gives me a look indicating that her current mode of transportation is completely inadequate due to her size."

"You should be a pet psychologist. I've never known anyone who could read animals like you do." Anne started the car and they made their way out onto the empty city streets. It had started to rain and everything was shiny as if covered in a thin coat of veneer.

"It would be a great job, except that you have to put up with owners. I'm not much for people, in case you haven't noticed."

Anne stopped at the light and then looked over at Hilton. "Now, let me get this straight. You live with three other women. You have two girlfriends and you like talk radio, which is all about people, but you don't like people." She studied Hilton's face.

This was as close to personal as she had gotten with Hilton. Despite being secretly curious about her, Anne hadn't managed to infiltrate her interior world. She kept her life, as Anne's father would say, close to the vest. This made her all the more intriguing.

"It doesn't mean I like people. One can be surrounded and yet remain remote."

Anne turned onto Elm Street. "Why remote?"

"You suffer less collateral damage that way."

"That's true." Anne saw the flashing red and blue lights at the end of the street. "That wouldn't happen to be your house, would it?"

"I think it is." Hilton screwed her face up in obvious consternation.

"Is this the logical end of every party?"

"No. Tonight is special."

"I have a really nice guest room. It's perfect for two."

"I wouldn't want to impose."

"Hilton, you wouldn't be imposing. Look, you need some sleep and I owe you breakfast. It'll be perfect."

Hilton was staring out the window. There were three police cars, and a crowd of women stood on the front lawn. Several of the neighbors had their lights on.

"Sounds wonderful. I really don't have the energy to deal with this right now."

"Good." Anne turned the corner and they left the crime scene behind them.

They didn't speak until they pulled up in front of Anne's one-story bungalow. Hilton gave Shannon the look, the kind Anne had seen mothers give their children before they went to a picky relative's house. "No hopping on the furniture, excessive tail wagging or muddy paw prints on the windowsills. Got it?"

Shannon barked.

"All right, let's go," Hilton said.

Anne opened the front door. "She'll be fine, really."

They walked inside. Shannon stood close to Hilton. "This is nice."

"Courtesy of my gay ex-husband. Always be suspicious of a man who can decorate, cook and do laundry better than you can. I should have known something wasn't right."

Anne watched as Hilton looked around. She tried to imagine what Hilton would think of it. It was tastefully decorated in dark brown leather furniture and lined with mahogany bookcases that contained leatherbound books grouped in sets and small brass trinkets placed throughout in order to accentuate the embossed gold titles of the books. On one wall was a large fireplace with a heavy, ornately carved mantel. She remembered the afternoon Gerald came home, his face flushed with excitement at having found the mantel at an estate sale. It had been horribly abused, but Gerald had restored it to its former condition, aside from a few irreparable nicks and scratches that he'd disguised as best he could. A thick Oriental rug finished off the room. He had spent months looking for that rug, making certain that the colors and the pattern went perfectly with the room. The windows had burgundy velvet curtains that were pulled back with gold cords.

Shannon looked up at Hilton as if looking for a clue to her next move.

"Let's get a beer," Anne said. She led them back to the kitchen, thinking that Shannon might be more comfortable there.

"Sure, I'm still kind of wired. I guess I'm worried about what's going on at the house, but at the same time I don't want to know. You see, remote is better. There's a crisis in my world but I'm not part of it."

Shannon lay down on the tile in the kitchen and let out what sounded to Anne like a sigh of relief.

The kitchen had a huge island in the middle of it and Hilton took a seat on one of the tall chairs. Shannon got up and went to look out the French doors. Hilton went with her.

"Oh, how nice. I like the deck," Hilton said. "Do you need to go out?" she asked Shannon. Apparently not, as Shannon lay down on the braided rug in front of the doors and seemed content.

"That's a good spot," Anne said. She never thought she'd be concerned about a dog guest but she was now. She pulled two Amstel Light beers from the rounded, retro, turquoise fridge. All the appliances in the kitchen were art deco colors and the walls were painted a light yellow.

"I didn't think they made this kind of stuff anymore," Hilton said, indicating the appliances.

"Neither did I, but Gerald found a company that makes all this stuff in southern California, so here we are in his dream kitchen."

"Is he like an interior designer or something?"

"Not yet but he'll probably end up being one. He works in marketing at the moment. It's kind of a progression—being straight, getting married and then deciding he liked boys." Anne took a sip of beer. She had yet to share any of this with anyone else.

She was just as guilty as Hilton when it came to playing it close to the vest. She didn't like people knowing too much about the things she truly held precious. Her pain was one of them. It was the one great failure of her life and it still burned even though a year and a half had passed. A first-year psych student could tell her that this was a bad plan and she probably did need some counseling, but to what end? She could pay someone to sit and listen in an office somewhere. She would use copious amounts of Kleenex while she told some bespectacled stranger that she was still angry and hurt. Instead, she told her pickle-heiress new friend and employee the worst story of her life.

"Yeah, that's pretty fucked up. It's not like you can hope to compete."

Anne laughed. "Not unless I miraculously sprouted a penis in the middle of the night."

"Like those sea monkey things that kids grow."

"What are those things exactly?" Anne asked.

"They're tiny brine shrimp. Have you been to therapy?" Hilton asked out of the blue.

"No. I mean, what's the point?" Anne was taken aback. They'd gone from shrimp to shrinks. "He's got his life and I've got mine."

"My father sent me to therapy for years. I don't think it accomplished much. I did a lot of coloring and we played games but that was about it." Hilton finished her beer.

"You want another one?"

"Sure."

"After your mother died?" Anne finished her beer and got them both another.

"Yeah, I guess they thought the trauma of seeing my mother dead on the beach was too much for a six-year-old. They never knew I helped her. We strapped the diving weights on together. She kissed me good-bye and then went off into the Sound. I knew she wasn't coming back. She was so unhappy except for that day. That day she was happy. I missed her but I can't help thinking she was better off."

Anne tried to imagine Hilton as a child standing there watching the whole thing—the disconnect must have begun at that very moment. Attempting to lighten the mood, knowing almost intrinsically that if she didn't she'd lose Hilton again to that remote place, she said, "So basically, you're saying therapy is stupid."

Hilton laughed. "Not exactly. We all need some psychic tweaking now and then. Therapists tell you what you already know but refuse to admit to yourself. So if you can get yourself to cowboy up you'll save yourself a ton of cash and keep a lot of tissue out of the landfill."

"Okay, I'll cowboy up. I'm pissed off that the love of my life dumped me. There, I said it."

"Do you feel better?"

"No."

"But you didn't waste a hundred bucks finding that out." Hilton took another swig of beer. Shannon rolled on her side and promptly fell asleep.

"Is that how much they charge?"

"A good one."

"Let's go sit in the living room. It's more comfortable. I think I'd take my hundred dollars and buy a nice shirt and a box of really expensive chocolates and that's how I'd feel better."

Hilton laughed again.

"What?" Anne asked. They both plopped down on the couch. Anne grabbed the remote and clicked on the gas fireplace.

"Sometimes you remind me so much of the woman who should be my girlfriend."

"Who's that?"

"My roommate Liz, the woman who brought you upstairs. She's all the things I admire and respect."

Anne kicked her shoes off and tucked her feet under her. "Can I ask you a personal question?"

"No."

Anne was momentarily stunned.

"I'm kidding. Shoot."

"What exactly is the deal with you and Natalie?"

"Boy, you had me freaked for a minute there. I thought you

were going to ask something serious." Hilton took off her sneakers, and Anne thought she might be starting to relax. She had the impression that Hilton didn't relax well. Hilton continued, "That's more like public information. Nat is basically a bitch-cunt-whore and I'm perfect."

Anne nearly choked on her beer.

This really made Hilton laugh. "No, really, we are each other's first loves and it's gone bad. We probably should call it quits, but we grew up together and it's hard to let go. Nat got thrown out of her house when she was fourteen and she came to live with Gran and me."

Anne put her beer down on the end table, being careful to use a coaster. It was one of Gerald's pet peeves and it still stuck with her. She positioned a pillow behind her head. Her neck was killing her. She needed to go to the chiropractor. She had one more question. It was one Gerald couldn't answer or wouldn't answer.

"You can ask it." Hilton met her gaze.

"Ask what?" Anne made a semi-gallant attempt, just for the sake of appearances, to look innocent. It failed. She could tell by the look of Hilton's face.

"It's the question every straight woman eventually asks a lesbian. How does it work? What happens to make you cross that line?"

"All right, I admit it. Gerald gave some lame excuse about how it just happened and one day he was in love with another man. I don't buy that."

"He's not completely off base. I think deep down we all have an inkling that something isn't quite right in the House of Straight. We play along for as long as we can until one day the right person with the right spark comes along and burns down the house. I just remember being sixteen and late one night Nat plants this kiss on me and tells me she's in love. Next thing I know all those weird feelings I had at soccer practice and those other intense strange friendships all make sense. I knew then that I liked women, but it took Nat's rash bravado to bring it all to the surface."

"What did your grandmother think about all this?"

63

"We never told her. I was twenty-four when she died and I never had a boyfriend. She knew." Hilton shrugged. "I don't think she really cared. She wasn't that fond of men herself. When she got sick I started to try and explain things but she stopped me. She said there were two things I must do—be happy, and if I ever did get married make damn sure the bastard signed a prenuptial agreement."

"Smart lady. So it really does just happen."

"If there's a seed . . ." Hilton yawned and rubbed her eyes.

"We better be done. Let's go get you and Shannon set up. Does she need a bowl of water?"

"Yeah, that's a good idea."

Anne got a bowl of water and they collected Shannon.

"You know she's going to sleep on the bed," Hilton said as they entered the guest room. Hilton stared at the tall rows of bookcases filled with tattered paperbacks that took up one wall of the room.

"And it's quite all right," Anne said.

She turned back to look at Anne. "The books in the living room were Gerald's and these are yours, correct?"

"You got it. I love mystery novels."

"It's quite a collection," Hilton said.

Anne pulled down the quilt and fluffed up the pillows. "Sleep tight, Hilton."

"You too."

Anne went to her own room and got undressed. She was glad she'd talked about Gerald tonight. Maybe she was healing. It was starting to feel like it wasn't her fault after all. Hilton was right—she couldn't have competed. And what sort of marriage would it have been if Gerald had persisted in living a lie? She lay down and adjusted the pillow so her neck didn't throb.

Chapter Six

Hilton ended up spending the next day with Anne. They went to Pike Street Market and added themselves to the throng of Saturday afternoon shoppers. Instead of breakfast, they went to Iver's Restaurant and had fried clams and fish and chips. Anne tried Hilton's fried clams and insinuated that they were batter-dipped rubber bands. Then they went shopping.

"What do you mean you don't understand how to buy clothes?" Anne asked.

They were standing in front of the Body Boutique, the sex toy store where the infamous purple dildo had no doubt been purchased. Anne insisted it had been purchased at a gag shop. Hilton was showing her otherwise.

"I just don't get it. I wear this stuff"—Hilton pointed to her camo-wear— "because I know it matches. I don't have to make any decisions."

"Like those little matching outfits they make for toddlers," Anne said brightly.

Hilton glared at her.

"I meant that in a nice way."

"So I'm textile-challenged. Do you want to go in and take a look around?"

"No! I don't think that's a good idea. Mind you, not that I'm afraid. I'm not, but I can just envision me getting spotted by one of my listeners and it gets all over town. I can see the news blurb now. Talk show host caught in dildo shop picking out the big one."

Hilton laughed. "I guess you've got a point there." The ad promo department at the radio station liked to use Anne's face in their local print ads, so local listeners knew her. She was extremely photogenic with her green eyes and neatly cut curly hair. Hilton was always fascinated with the fact that all the rain and humidity in Seattle only seemed to make Anne's hair look better. It played havoc with her long hair, giving it fits of fly-away strands and giant snarls. She was endlessly threatening to get it cut off.

"I have a better idea."

"Yes?"

"Let's go get you some clothes, real clothes."

Hilton raised an eyebrow.

"I'm not being like Veronica," Anne said. She raised her right hand. "I swear. Hilton, you're gorgeous. You have a nice figure. Good clothes would really do you justice. I mean, so-called camowear can only take you so far."

Hilton smiled. "You're lucky I'm not offended."

"I wasn't offended by eating fried rubber bands."

"I was just trying to broaden your horizons," Hilton said. "I could go shopping. You know, Gran wasn't much into the physical side of life so I never really learned those things that other girls did. I always felt a little backward in the girly department."

Anne took Hilton's hand. "Come on. Class is now in session."

They went back to the car where they found a small crowd gathered around Anne's Chevy Avalanche. Shannon was sitting in the front seat giving the impression that she was driving. People were laughing and Shannon had that panting dog smile that makes humans anthropomorphize them. Hilton made her move. "You big ham."

Shannon climbed in the backseat and Hilton gave her a french fry that she'd saved from lunch.

Later that evening, Anne dropped Hilton and Shannon off with six shopping bags full of clothes, which didn't account for the outfit Hilton was wearing. It occurred to Hilton that she hadn't been home in nearly twenty-four hours. She slipped in the front door, hoping that all was quiet and that Nat had gone out. To her surprise Jessie was sitting in the living room watching a movie with a small, brown teddy bear next to her. The bear was wrapped up in a blanket. Her biology book was draped carelessly over her leg. This constituted studying in Jessie's world, which was why she was endlessly on academic probation.

"What's up?" Hilton said as she set the shopping bags on the floor.

"Not much. What's up with you? You're all fixed up. What happened to camo-girl?"

"She's been laid to rest. Anne took me shopping." Hilton blushed involuntarily. She hoped Jessie wouldn't notice. No such luck.

"Yeah, what is up with you and the boss lady? You've been gone since last night. I've told you about not making your bread where you eat your meat."

"That's so disgusting and it's not like that." Hilton sat on the couch and slipped off her new Italian leather boots.

Jessie raised an eyebrow. "Not yet. Anyway, you missed all the excitement with the cops."

"Not exactly. We drove past and kept on going. What happened?"

"Nat and Emily got into a catfight in the front yard and someone called the cops. Nobody got hurt. The cops broke it up and made everyone go home."

"Is Nat with the biker chick?"

"Yeah, man, Nat's really freaking lately. I mean, she's not usually like this."

"I think Nat's falling in love and doing her best to ignore the fact. You know how she is."

"It'll probably pass, like all the others," Jessie said sagely. She pulled the blanket up higher on the bear and patted its head maternally.

"Jessie, what's going on with the bear?"

"Oh, I'm bear-sitting. Remember the night I tried to set Liz up with what I thought was the perfect girlfriend?"

Hilton drew a blank.

"You know, the night of your little indiscretion with Emily."

It all came back to her in vivid color—pink hair, rocking hips, languid, wet kisses. Then she remembered the pretty blonde on the couch with the bear. "The one who looked just like Barbie's friend Skipper?"

"Yeah, her name is Melissa. Liz and Melissa did end up talking and now they're out on a date."

"Really?"

"Is that wicked or what? So I offered to bear-sit. I wanted them to have some quality time."

"How come Liz didn't tell me?" Hilton was kind of hurt at being left out of the loop.

"Uh, because you were gone," Jessie ventured.

"Oh, yeah."

Shannon whined.

"Okay, I guess you might be hungry. You want an egg sandwich?"

Shannon barked.

"Then come back and show me your new outfits. You look hot."

Hilton smiled. "Sure."

❧

Hilton fixed Shannon an egg sandwich and then went back to the living room to cut tags and organize her purchases. Anne had taken her to this woman's store where they found the most amazing things. "I mean, look at this," Hilton said, holding up a coffee-colored short suede jacket with braided trim. She had a ruffled paisley blouse of deep reds and browns to wear under it and a pair of dark brown hipster polyester pants.

"Wow, that is beautiful. This is not your regular department store stuff." Jessie put the blouse on over her T-shirt. "I'm thinking lots of cash."

"But it's quality. I don't know, it's some kind of rich lady store where they have all this designer stuff and the saleswoman helps you pick it out and you look great when she's done with you. Anne shops there."

"Nice suit," Jessie said, holding it up. It was a black leather suit with a white silk collared shirt. The pants were boot-cut and had sterling silver rivets. "It looks like something Johnny Cash would wear. Go try it on."

They spent the rest of the evening with the fashion show and then watched the remainder of the *Brother Bear* video.

"Kids' videos rock sometimes," Jessie said. She grabbed a handful of popcorn and shoved it in her mouth.

"Why's that?" Hilton asked.

"It's that feel-good stuff."

Hilton scratched Shannon's ears. "But there's no sex."

Jessie laughed. "Not everything I do has sex in it."

Hilton scoffed. "Almost everything you do. Come on, Jessie, getting laid makes your world go around."

"Well, it does play an important role," Jessie conceded.

Hilton rolled her eyes. "Okay, I'm calling it a night. Are you going to wait up?"

"Of course, I want to get all the details. I'm going to put Amelia Bearhart to bed and then watch the episodes of *the L word* that I taped. As a small bear-child she really shouldn't be watching smut."

Hilton gave her an I-told-you-so look and went off to bed with Shannon. It was a full moon, she noticed as the two of them made their way across the lawn. The lawn was slowly turning a brownish yellow and the dogwood trees were still littering the flower beds with their dark burgundy leaves. The fall had been a pretty one, full of sunshine and cool mornings. When the drier weather came it would do wonders for her hair and she'd be able to get away with brushing it once in the morning and once before bed.

Over the back fence she could see little hanging pumpkin lights on her neighbor's veranda. They were always decorating for the holidays. It would be Halloween in two weeks and she was kind of glad Nat wasn't around because the big Halloween party wouldn't be taking place this year. Hilton had already declined the Queer Nation people's request to host the party. She, Jessie and Liz had tentatively made plans to hang out together and watch cheesy black-and-white horror films and carve pumpkins. Hilton was kind of hoping she could convince Anne to come over, if she wasn't busy.

She opened the door to the cottage and Shannon jumped on the bed, letting out a heavy sigh. "I know, girl. I'm pretty beat myself."

Hilton disrobed and carefully hung up her new clothes. Anne had mentioned something about dry cleaning. She eyed her new clothes with suspicion. They were starting to resemble a commitment.

On Monday morning, Veronica fawned over her, admiring Hilton's new look. She had brought her a second cup of coffee and wanted to know what she was doing for lunch. The control room always seemed a little crowded when Veronica was in there fussing around. Hilton could tell Dave was as uncomfortable as she was. He kept moving his elbows in a funny way like he needed more room.

"I've got to take Shannon to the vet for her annual shots."

Shannon's ears perked up a bit.

"Some other time then," Veronica said as she floated off.

Anne had apparently seen the whole thing. "Well, well, well, aren't we suddenly popular." She stood in the doorway of the control room.

"A little too popular," Hilton grumbled. She had spent more than her usual amount of time getting ready because now she had to make choices. She had finally decided on a turquoise, big, collared blouse and black hipster trousers. She felt kind of funny getting dressed up but this was what businesswomen did, and she was a grownup now.

"I told you blue looked good on you," Anne said, coming in the room and straightening out the back of Hilton's collar.

"And you should have mentioned La Femme Nikita would be after me if I wore it."

"It slipped my mind."

"Dude, you really look hot," Dave chimed in.

"Thanks," Hilton said, pointedly turning to her computer and checking out the Web site.

"Did you notice the footwear?" Anne said.

"Expensive," Dave said, indicating Hilton's leather boots. "Does she have new socks too?"

"As a matter of fact, she does. Say bye-bye to cheap white gym socks."

"Off white," Hilton corrected.

"We do have to work on your laundry skills. It's called bleach."

"I'm the sniff-and-toss girl, remember? But enough about me," Hilton said.

Lillian came in the office wearing a pink brocade skirt and jacket outfit with a dazzling white hat that was the size of a turkey platter.

"Good morning, Lillian," Anne said.

"Who's the new girl? I was just getting used to GI Jane and now you've gone and changed everything."

"No, Lillian, it's still Hilton," Anne said cheerfully.

Lillian leaned down and peered at her. "Good God, you're right. You almost look like a girl."

Lillian's faded blue eyes looked like the size of tea saucers behind her Coke bottle lenses. She backed away and went to her desk on the opposite side of the control room, obviously satisfied that Hilton was still Hilton.

Veronica brought Hilton another cup of coffee.

"Thank you, Veronica, but I really can't. I don't have anything in my stomach and it's starting to hurt."

"Why didn't you say something? I'll go and get you a Smoothie at the shop downstairs." Shoving the coffee at Anne, she darted off before Hilton had a chance to stop her.

"Don't mind if I do," Anne said, taking a sip.

"She never brings me coffee," Dave whined.

Hilton laughed. "Next time she comes by I'll mention it."

Lillian sat at her desk and then read the day's agenda, or attempted to as she adjusted and readjusted her glasses. "Great guns! We're starting the day off with a glaring typo," she shouted.

"Excuse me?" Anne said. She was staring over Hilton's shoulder at the Web site.

"It says here we're going to talk about God's place in our society. You mean dogs, right? Like leash laws and picking up dog crap on the city streets. Did I ever tell you the time when my sister and I went to Paris with a bunch of old biddies from her Methodist church? I never met a more boring, uptight, nervous group of Ex-Laxers in my whole life. I swore that if I saw one more crochet hook I'd scream. What! The afghan can't wait? Who knits her way across Europe? Anyway, I saw the Eiffel Tower—looks like an overblown Erector set—but the most amazing thing was the motorcycle with a big tank on the back. They vacuumed up the dog poop. Those French people—ingenious bunch. Well, and we've always known how squeamish they are—wouldn't want a little doo-doo on their freshly perfumed hands."

Hilton was staring at Lillian in awe. Anne was obviously used to these tangential diatribes because she didn't appear to be the least bit bothered by it.

"I'm thinking we should get Lillian her own show. We wouldn't even need callers. We could do the whole show by word association. It would rock," Dave said, running his fingers though his messy brown hair.

Anne scowled at him. "Where's your loyalty?"

"It's radio, we're always looking for the next best thing. Man, I got to move up if I'm going to support the Gucci habit my new girl has."

Anne glared at him and then said, "No, Lillian, it's about God, G-O-D. You know how God is slowly being removed from the schools, from holidays, from court buildings and finally the Pledge of Allegiance. We can't teach the Declaration of Independence because it mentions God too many times. Come on, if I was God, I'd be pissed off. I just don't get it."

Lillian frowned. "Next thing you know you'll be getting the crochet needles out just like those old biddy Methodists my sister is so fond of."

"Just take calls from people who want to talk about God and politics."

"Next you'll be having prayer services before the show and we'll all be going on retreat together," Lillian muttered.

Anne rolled her eyes and left for her own booth. The intro music started. Today, Dave chose an old show tune by Frank Sinatra. Anne smiled as Sinatra belted out the last line of, "My Way."

Anne laughed. She switched on the mike. "How appropriate."

Dave gave her the thumbs-up. He switched on station identification KCOM-FM and the promo part of Anne's show. Hilton zoomed in on Anne's face and did some last-minute adjustments. Lillian put her headphones on and Veronica peeked in to ensure all was well. Hilton loved this moment. It was showtime.

Anne studied her notes and then started her monologue. "Today, we're going to begin the show with a hypothetical situation. Now, say you design, implement and fund your very own corporation. You get it up and running, put people in charge—make everything all fine and nice. You own one hundred percent of the

73

stock. It's all going so well until one day something starts to change. It's undermining. Say it starts in the mailroom with the clerks. They start reinterpreting the incoming mail. They start translating your words into their own language—a language you don't speak. They tell you it's just a form of corporate shorthand, a better way to communicate with the rest of the group. You, as head honcho, get a little nervous, feel a little unease in your gut, but the workers and middle management seem to be running smoothly. You take a trip and you come back to find upper management has changed the credo. There's a hostile takeover. They set you up and bam! You're out the door of your corporation. The boxes are packed, your last check is cut and you're history. You're so shocked and dismayed that you forget to protest. It's not until later that it all becomes apparent what they've done. They've rewritten, reinvented and reconstituted you, and then to add insult to injury they slowly begin to remove you from society. That's what really sucks. Now, you're expendable. Every holiday, every word, every mention of you is to be eradicated as if you never existed. What would you do? How would you feel? Now, you might be thinking this is some big guy that has it all and he just got the shaft. So who cares? And you'd be correct. But what if the big corporate executive is God? I'm thinking we all better watch out because if the one in charge decides to exact a little retribution we're in big trouble."

Hilton watched the computer monitor. Anne was totally brilliant. At the moment she looked like a television evangelist getting really serious just before he asks for your wallet. She looked stunning in her dark green gabardine tailored suit with a black silk shirt. The combination of green and black set off her green eyes and seemed to accent her dark curls. Her hair was cut just above her chin and hung loosely around her face. Hilton swore she must get her hair trimmed every other week because it always looked perfect, unlike her own snarled mess. It was drizzling outside and her hair was a disaster. She tied it up in disgust. She'd come up with various methods for twisting it around and sort of tucking it back into itself. If she didn't move around a lot it would stay that way for a while.

Break came and Anne clicked on her mike. "How was that?"

"Beautiful, for a minute there I thought you'd morphed into Dr. Jerry Falwell. It kind of scared me," Hilton said. "Come take a look at it."

"I have better hair than he does," she said, taking her hand and fluffing up her curls.

Lillian was digging around in her beige purse for her cigarettes. Hilton had watched this scene for several days in a row, wondering what Lillian could possibly be hauling around in a purse that was the size of a suitcase and why she always lost her cigarettes in its enormous void. When Anne entered the room Lillian said, "There's a bunch of kook balls on the line that want to talk this and that."

"Lillian, could you be a little more specific?" Anne said as she came into the control room.

"Kooks about you-know-who," Lillian said, pointing upward.

"About G-O-D?"

"Yes, I'll be surprised if my sister doesn't pop in with a brief commentary."

"Maybe we should call her," Anne said. She sat on the corner of Hilton's desk and eyed the video stream coming in on the computer monitor. Hilton hit playback so Anne could see the last segment. She felt her presence acutely and for half a second she wondered if Jessie was right. Did she have a thing for her boss? She instantly dismissed it. It was an atypical response to an atypical situation. And it was all typical nonsense. She liked Anne. She thought she was brilliant and funny, but lust and infatuation were just figments of Jessie's overactive imagination.

"Call my sister, hell no! That woman could talk the ear off an elephant. I'd never get her off the line. Did I ever tell you the time we went to the Portland Zoo . . ."

"Lillian, if you want to smoke, you'd better get going," Anne said, pointing to the big black clock. They had approximately six minutes before Anne had to be back on the air.

Anne's show ran from ten in the morning until twelve. Each segment was approximately fifteen minutes long. At every quarter hour they broke for commercials, news and weather. This was the perfect length of time for Hilton to keep the Web site updated and not get burned out sitting endlessly in front of the computer.

"Oh, crap. I'll tell you later," Lillian said. She bustled off as fast as her square-heeled orthopedic shoes would carry her.

"That was good," Dave said. He got up and stretched.

"And the rest of the day will be even better," Anne said, rubbing her hands together gleefully. "Do you want to go to lunch after the show?"

"I'd love to but I have to take Shannon to get her annual shots. It doesn't take long. You could come with and then we could go eat."

Dave gave them both a funny look.

"Dave, would you like to go to lunch too?" Anne asked.

"I wasn't invited."

"Dave, you're acting like a girl."

"Dude, I was just messing with you. Actually, I got a date with the new mail clerk downstairs."

"The one with the Gucci obsession?" Anne inquired.

"Have you seen her?" Dave asked.

"Those are not real," Anne said.

Hilton smirked. It was obvious that the woman had breast implants.

"Does it really matter?" he replied, his eyes glossing over.

"I think he's visualizing his face nestled between them," Anne said to Hilton.

"Was I that obvious?" he asked.

Anne glanced at the clock. "Yes, and try to remember not to stare at her chest the whole time you're having lunch. It's a dead giveaway."

"Dude, it'll be seriously hard."

"Try," Hilton advised. "You'll get to that place faster if you pretend to be interested in her mind. Remember, you're not the only guy on the planet who wants to rent the condo with nipples."

"Got it."

"Condo with nipples?" Anne clicked in from her booth.

"You weren't supposed to hear that," Hilton replied.

Dave started the bumper music and played "Brick House."

Lillian came clunking in and the show began.

Anne interspersed the second segment of the show with pro and con calls. There was much heated debate and Anne pretty much let the callers do all the work. She engaged in one of her favorite pastimes, which was throwing pencils at the suspended fiberglass ceiling. There must have been a thousand pencils up there already. Every now and again, Ed would have maintenance change out the panels, he'd have a discussion with her about her proclivity, and then it would continue. No one had lost an eye yet.

Veronica came flying into the control room all out breath. "Great goodness, you wouldn't think getting a smoothie would be so difficult. It seems there's some kind of fruit dispute and it's suddenly extremely hard to come by. It's a dock strike or something."

"Veronica, you didn't have to go to all that trouble, really." Hilton almost felt guilty. She did feel a little more confident, a little more in control. Attitude was everything and good clothes seem to help even if her hair was fucked up.

"You've got to keep your energy up."

"Thank you," Hilton said, taking a sip. Shannon woke up from her mid-morning nap and came sauntering over to check it out. Hilton gave her a taste.

Dave was busy making it look like he was fainting from famine but Veronica pointedly ignored him. He must have been somewhat convincing because Shannon came over and licked his face. Dave giggled and screamed.

Anne clicked on her mike from the radio booth as station identification played. "We need to get him a man or a testosterone shot. He's acting like a girl again."

Dave managed to extricate himself from Shannon and stood up. He grabbed his balls and said, "No way. I'm man, all man."

"Whatever," Anne said, rolling her eyes. She was back on the air.

Hilton was enjoying the show when Natalie arrived. Anne was having an animated conversation with a fervent atheist. Somehow Nat had wheedled her way past Veronica, which for Nat wouldn't have been that difficult, Hilton thought. Nat could charm the smock off a nun if it was to her advantage. In fact, she probably had.

Hilton opened the door to the control room. "What are you doing here?" she asked. She stood in the doorway to block Nat's entrance. Suddenly, she was concerned because Nat didn't do things like show up at work. Half the time Nat had no idea where she was. They just sort of ran into each other whenever. They were actually more like sisters than lovers. Still, what love and sex and lust was between them hadn't found a place to go or a way to end.

"I came to talk to you. I'm moving to Sherry's for a little while." Nat pulled her knapsack up on her shoulder. It looked heavy and Hilton figured it was full of clothes. Not a lot, but enough to indicate this wasn't an overnighter.

"What! You're moving out?" Hilton could feel her heart pounding in her ears like the way waves make that thudding sound when they hit the beach.

"I just think it'll be better if I wasn't around while you're having this thing with that pink-haired freak, Emily." Nat peered into the booth at Anne who was twirling a pencil between her fingers like a baton.

"Nat, I'm not doing anything with Emily. I haven't seen her since that night. You've seen more of her than I have. Really, I'm not that interested. You know, it was kind of a one-time thing." Hilton realized she was pleading. Part of her was totally disgusted. After all, it was Nat who did most of the messing around. The other part of her was cringing in the corner with terror that the one person in her life masquerading as a constant was about to make a run for it.

"I always wondered what she looked like," Nat said, apparently more interested in Anne than in the fact she was tearing Hilton's world apart. She was like a child who'd spent all afternoon meticulously building a house with wooden blocks only to kick them all over in a gleeful act of total destruction.

"Nat, could we talk about us for a minute? You can't just move out like this. What about us?" Hilton whispered. Dave was doing his best to pretend he wasn't in the room.

"Oh, it'll be fine. I'm sure I'll be back before you know it. You know how I am." Nat touched her cheek. "I love you."

Shannon came up behind her and peed on Nat's pant leg.

Nat swung around. "Damn it! Why does she do that to me?"

"Because she can tell you're upsetting me." Hilton went and sat down in her chair. She could tell there was no reasoning with Nat. She had made her decision and now it was time for action. That was one of the things Hilton admired yet despised about her. What was done was done and what needed to be done was done regardless of how foolish or destructive the choice became.

"I've got to go. Sherry is waiting for me downstairs."

"Great! Tell her hi for me," Hilton said facetiously. She doubted Nat would get it. She never did.

Hilton watched her go and then got up, kicked her chair and went to the restroom.

She had her face in the sink and was running cold water over her eyes when Anne found her. Dave must have informed her.

"Are you all right?" Anne asked.

"Yeah." Hilton dried her face. Her eyes were red and it was apparent she'd been crying.

"Was that Natalie?"

"Yeah, she's going to move out for a while."

"Oh."

"I guess I should have seen that one coming. I'm not good at seeing her sucker punches coming. You'd think I would be."

"Did Shannon pee on her?"

Hilton smiled weakly. "Yeah, she does that sometimes."

Anne started to laugh then contained herself. Then Hilton laughed.

"Got to love that dog," Anne said.

"She's better than any girlfriend I've had."

"Which is pretty much Nat."

"Well, yeah."

"Can you get her to do that on command?"

"I don't know. Why?" Hilton grabbed some toilet paper and blew her nose. There was no sense pretending she hadn't been crying. Besides, with Anne somehow it didn't matter. Anne knew what it was like to lose someone. Nat had hurt her and then she had a good little cry. She didn't need to be ashamed. Sometimes she wished she had more normal people skills like Anne. Anne could handle any situation. Hilton always felt kind of awkward. She thought one day she might outgrow her social phobias but that had yet to happen. She often wondered if it ever would.

"Because I'd like to take her to the monthly staff meeting and have her pee on people who are giving me a hard time."

Hilton laughed.

Anne gave her a hug. "In a couple of days you'll feel better and you'll get more logical about it. I swear." Anne held her for a minute longer than was probably necessary but neither of them pulled away. There was a knock at the door and they both jumped.

It was Dave. "Dudes, it's, like, almost time."

"I hate when he calls me a dude."

"It's kind of like a term of endearment," Hilton replied.

"I'll take you to lunch after our vet visit and we'll have a couple of adult beverages and you'll feel better."

Hilton nodded. They had one more half-hour segment. Hilton was glad. She'd have some time to compose herself.

After the show, they took Shannon to the vet in Anne's Chevy Avalanche. It appeared Shannon thought they were going for a ride until they got closer to the vet's office. She must have memorized its location because she started to whimper and whine the closer they got. Then she started pacing in the backseat. When Hilton pulled the leash out of her backpack, Shannon barked. She was seldom on a leash, so when it appeared, she knew for certain where they were going.

"Stop being such a baby. You think going for a pelvic exam is a treat and I still do it. It'll take five minutes. I thought you liked Dr. Vincente."

Shannon whimpered again.

"This is sad," Anne said, looking into the rearview mirror.

"Don't buy into it. It's quick and it's necessary. I'm glad you came, though. Sometimes I have a little trouble getting her into the office."

"Trouble?" Anne said, pulling into the parking lot Hilton had pointed to.

"You'll see."

It started with trying to get Shannon out of the backseat. Hilton had Anne hold Shannon's leash from the other direction while she pushed her. Hilton took hold of the leash and then she pulled and Anne pushed Shannon to the front door. Shirley, the vet tech, opened the door. She took the leash and Anne and Hilton pushed Shannon through the door.

"There is a downside to having big dogs," Shirley said. She wiped a bead of sweat off the end of her nose. She was a petite, curly-headed redhead and Hilton had always admired her skill with animals. Shirley pulled a piece of dried black meat from her pocket. Shannon became a different dog instantly. She sat down and patiently waited for her treat.

"Do you have any more of those?" Hilton asked.

"We just got a shipment in. I saved two bags for you. You can buy one and your friend can buy one," Shirley said, winking at them.

"Are they a precious commodity?" Anne inquired as they followed Shirley into the examination room.

"They are if you're a dog and there's a limit of one bag per customer," Hilton explained.

"What are they?"

"They're air-dried, grass-fed buffalo livers."

"Yum," Anne said.

"Dogs will do anything for them," Shirley said as she prepared the vaccinations for the vet.

Dr. Vincente came in. She was a tall, leggy blonde with her hair pulled back in a bun. She wore purple scrubs and faded black high-top sneakers. She held out her hand and Shannon came over and licked.

"See, this isn't so bad," Hilton said.

Dr. Vicente smiled at Hilton. "Had a bit of a time getting her in here."

"Just a little," Hilton replied. "Luckily, I had help."

"Aren't you Anne Counterman?" Dr. Vicente asked, staring intently at her.

"Yes."

"We listen to your show every morning in the office. My goodness, you're absolutely hysterical and right on target."

"Why, thank you," Anne said.

Hilton noticed that Anne blushed slightly at the compliment.

"Well, Shannon, don't we have important and famous friends." Dr. Vicente scratched her ears and fed her another piece of buffalo liver. She gently inserted the needle beneath Shannon's scruff. Judging from her lack of response, she must not have felt a thing. Dr. Vicente looked in her ears, listened to her heart and pronounced her fit.

Shannon bounded out of the exam room but kept a close eye on Anne and the two bags of buffalo livers. Hilton was writing a check at the reception counter while Anne was inspecting the display of dried things that dogs liked. She picked up one that looked like a long brown cigar. She ran it under her nose like a cigar.

"What's this?" she asked, taking a closer look.

"It looks like one of those rawhide chewy things," Hilton ventured.

"Actually, it's a dried bull penis," Shirley said as she handed Hilton her receipt.

Anne dropped it instantly. She was clearly aghast.

"It seems to have that effect on a lot of people," Shirley said diplomatically.

"I think I'll wash my hands."

Shirley and Hilton waited until she was out of earshot before they exploded into giggles.

"Parts are parts, I guess," Hilton said.

"We had one woman in here who bought a half-dozen because she wanted to make her husband uncomfortable."

"I bet we'll hear about the bull penis episode on the show tomorrow," Hilton said.

"Nothing like free advertising," Shirley said.

"If they don't have a pet with them, don't let them in," Hilton warned. "They will have only come to see the oddities on display."

Anne looked relieved now that she had washed her hands. She gave the jar of bull penises a dirty look on the way out the door. When they got to the car, Anne said, "You know, for hanging out with a lesbian I've sure had a lot of exposure to male genitalia lately."

Hilton just smiled. "Where are we going for lunch?"

"You pick." Anne started the car and Shannon let out an audible sigh.

"She'll sleep now. Let's go somewhere horribly decadent."

"I know just the place. It's a fondue bar, nice quiet booths, great food and wine list, and the desserts are to die for."

"Will I be drowning my sorrows like a straight girl?"

"You will." Anne pulled into traffic and headed downtown to the restaurant. The fog that had hovered over the city most of the morning had lifted and a seldom seen but much admired blue sky permeated the afternoon.

Hilton looked over at Anne and smiled. Maybe today wouldn't be a total wash after all. It was funny to think that she'd rather spend the afternoon with Anne than Nat anyway. So what did that really say about their relationship? she wondered. Maybe it was time to cut the cord.

Chapter Seven

When Hilton got home it was early evening. Shannon was still groggy from the shots. Hilton was satiated. She felt kind of tipsy, very full and in general not doing bad for someone who'd just lost her girlfriend.

"So you're doing better?" Anne had asked as she dropped her off.

"Much better, thank you."

"I'll zip by in the morning and pick you up. Your car will be safe in the parking garage."

"And I shouldn't be driving anyway," Hilton said. She looked at Anne a little longer than she should. "You're a nice lady."

"And you in your new duds are one hot mama."

"Anne!"

"Sorry, I must have morphed into Dave for a moment there. I'll see you tomorrow at eight-thirty."

Shannon was scratching at the door by the time Hilton got up the steps. "All right, all ready, I'm coming." She opened the door and flounced down on the couch with Jessie and Liz, who were once again watching reruns of *Leave it to Beaver* on cable television. It appeared they had been studying. Liz's books were piled neatly on the coffee table with yellow Post-it notes sticking out everywhere. Jessie's books were scattered on the floor with no apparent organization. Hilton banged her head on the back of the couch for emphasis. "Why do you guys watch this show?"

Liz smiled benevolently. "Because it's like going to another planet where everything works out." She took Hilton's hand. "Are you all right?"

"You mean because I got dumped?"

"I don't know if you necessarily got dumped," Liz said.

"Dude, you've totally got to do something about Emily," Jessie piped in.

Hilton saw Liz shoot her a dirty look.

"Why?"

"Because she's been looking for you. I mean, what's the deal? Are you doing her or not? Nat sure thinks you are." Jessie thrust her hand in an oversized bag of Cheetos. Her fingers were stained orange. She popped a handful in her mouth.

"I don't think those things are really food," Liz commented.

"Of course they're food," Jessie said defensively.

"No, I think they're a bunch of chemicals they glued together and labeled snack food," Liz said.

Shannon nuzzled Jessie for one.

"Don't give her one," Hilton said, giving her a stern look.

"Why not?"

"They're bad for you."

"God damn food nazis," Jessie grumbled. She slipped one to Shannon when she thought Hilton wasn't looking.

"I saw that."

"One won't hurt her. She's a big dog and the chemicals will be diluted. Now, about Emily."

"I don't know. Can't I just leave it a two-night stand? Is it necessary that every lesbian sexual liaison must turn into a three-year relationship that will be dysfunctional from its very inception? I don't think I'm in the mood to be in love." Hilton absentmindedly grabbed a Cheeto and stuck it in her mouth.

"Ah-ha! You ate one," Jessie said, pointing an accusing finger at her.

"They're not bad actually."

"You know why you don't want to fall for Emily?" Jessie said.

"No, I don't." She had replayed the evenings of their amorous liaison and had nice thoughts about it. Emily was sweet and sexy but that was about it. She wasn't horribly interesting or driven or funny. For the first time in her life, Hilton was looking for something with a future and it wasn't Emily.

"Hilton, should you be taking advice from the most relationship-challenged lesbian on the planet?" Liz piped in.

"Probably not. I should just settle down with you." Hilton took Liz's hand. "But I hear you've been dating someone."

"Maybe," Liz said coyly.

Jessie cleared her throat. "As I was saying, you're not interested in Emily because you've got a thing for your boss."

"Really?" Liz asked Hilton.

"Consider the source," Hilton said. She didn't meet Liz's gaze.

"Where have you been spending all your time?"

"Doing work-related activities," Hilton said. She grabbed another Cheeto and tried to appear nonchalant. "I think these things are addictive." Shannon looked at her pleadingly. She gave her another. They would both die of toxic chemicals.

Jessie continued, "And after work, part of a weekend and those shopping trips . . ."

"You're high. She's my boss, for starters."

"Like that ever stopped anyone."

"And she's straight."

"And her husband left her for another man. That should tell you something," Jessie countered.

86

"Like what?"

"Did he really leave her for a man?" Liz said, apparently shocked by this tidbit.

"Well, yeah," Hilton admitted.

"You know what that tells me?" Jessie said.

"Oh, do share." Hilton grabbed the afghan from the back of the couch and covered up with it. She was suddenly cold and kind of sleepy. The wine from lunch must have been wearing off or she was having a reaction to the Cheetos.

"It means that the house wasn't the same as all the other houses on the block. A woman doesn't marry a guy that turns gay. He was gay when she married him and they both knew it. Underneath all that playing it straight is a fag and dyke pretending to play house. It was only a matter of time before one of them broke the deal, found someone to love and went to live happily ever after somewhere in Homoslavia."

"You're so full of shit."

"Oh, my God, I've to go," Liz said, popping up. "I've got a date with Melissa at seven-thirty."

"Do I get to bear-sit?"

"No, Jessie, tonight we're having dinner at her place with Amelia Bearhart."

"Damn!"

"Another time." Liz patted Jessie's shoulder. "You are a good baby-sitter." Liz rolled her eyes at Hilton, who smirked.

"Like when?" Jessie whined.

"I'll see if you can take her to the park tomorrow. We have a lunch date."

"I'll pencil you in," Jessie said. She took a swig of orange soda and picked up the remote.

"Better hit the wine cellar for something nice," Hilton suggested.

"Can I?" Liz asked.

"Of course. Nothing like a good bottle of wine to enhance a

dinner date." Hilton pulled the afghan off. Now she was hot. Maybe she was really having a reaction to all those toxic chemicals in the junk food.

"What should I get?" Liz said. She looked tentatively at Hilton.

"Come on, I'll help you pick one out."

Hilton and Liz tromped downstairs to the wine cellar. It was originally a root cellar, but Gran had the whole thing redone with state-of-the-art equipment. Gran may have been frugal about some things but a good wine cellar was a priority. Gran had carefully cataloged brands and types. Hilton kept it religiously stocked. She disappeared into the dark corners of the cellar and came back with a dusty bottle of French wine. Liz blew off the label.

"This looks expensive."

"And tonight is a special occasion," Hilton said. She didn't have the heart to tell Liz that everything in the wine cellar was horribly expensive. What did it matter when you were a pickle heiress?

"Thank you, Hilton." Liz gave her a quick hug.

"So you really like this girl?" Hilton queried.

"I do. Melissa is different. I mean aside from the bear thing, she's sensitive, intuitive and very smart. Plus she's really cute."

"The bear's okay. We've all got our little idiosyncrasies. Besides, you've got a built-in baby-sitter." Hilton looked at Liz. She was gorgeous. Tonight she was wearing a soft, light green sweater with a cream-colored blouse and brown slacks. She looked elegantly casual. Her long brown hair was hanging perfectly over her shoulders.

"I don't get what's up with Jessie and the bear, but it's working."

"It's nice to see her focused on something other than her crotch."

"You can that say again. I can do this, right?" Liz asked with trepidation in her voice.

"Of course you can."

"Okay, well, here goes," Liz said. She straightened her shoulders and they both climbed the stairs back to the world of light and bears.

The next day, while Anne was doing her monologue about the bull penis, Jessie came racing into the control room at warp speed with Veronica nipping at her heels, telling her she wasn't allowed in here.

Jessie was carrying Amelia Bearhart's little leather aviator's jacket. "I don't think you understand the gravity of this emergency. There's been a kidnapping, or rather a bearnapping, and I need Hilton's help," she said, wildly waving the jacket around for emphasis.

Hilton, Dave and Lillian turned around to see Jessie flapping the tiny jacket around and arguing with Veronica. Jessie was dressed in her usual gym attire, a black Nike warm-up suit. Her short hair was wet around the temples like she'd been running.

When she saw Hilton, Jessie said, "You've got to totally help me. Someone took the bear. I need Shannon. She can, like, follow the scent. Thank God, I've still got the jacket." She held it to her breast.

"Hilton, she can't be in here," Veronica said, putting her hands on her hips. "Come outside and we'll discuss the situation. Dave, keep on eye on the Web site."

"Yes, ma'am."

Once they'd exited, Hilton shut the control room door. She figured Veronica would be on her way now that Jessie had been removed from sacred ground. Instead, she stood waiting for Jessie's explanation. Hilton got the ball rolling. "Now tell me what happened."

"I was bear-sitting and I took her to the park. She was sitting on the bench by the playground, you know, by those slides and swingsets. This loose dog came by and this really hot chick was chasing him. I went to help and when I got back the bear was gone. What the hell am I going to do?" Jessie began waving the jacket around again. "Liz is going to kill me. I knew I shouldn't have taken on so much responsibility. I'm incapable."

Jessie looked so distraught that even hard-hearted Veronica seemed suddenly compassionate.

"Melissa will break up with Liz because she doesn't have the bear, and I will be solely responsible for destroying their one chance at happiness."

Dave slipped out of the control room. "Dude, boss lady wants to know what's going on."

"Tell her my roommate Jessie lost her teddy bear and she wants Shannon to do a little detective work," Hilton explained. Dave gave her an odd look and went back inside to relay the information.

Jessie was staring at Hilton intently.

Hilton let out a heavy sigh. "Jessie, Shannon isn't a bloodhound. She doesn't know how to track things."

"Well, can't she give it a try? All dogs have good sniffers." Jessie held it out for Shannon, who gave it a perfunctory sniff and then went back to her fleece and brocade bed, a gift from Anne, and went back to sleep. It appeared the crisis was cutting into her nap time. "Hilton, you've got to help me," Jessie pleaded.

"I'm going to. Now, what park were you at?"

"The one on Lincoln and Central."

"What time?" Hilton asked. She noticed that Veronica had produced a small black notebook from the pocket of her blazer and was jotting this down.

"Twelve-thirty."

"What was Amelia wearing?" Hilton asked.

"Nothing! I took off her jacket because she looked kind of warm. I figured with her fur and shit. Oh, fuck, she's gone missing and she's naked."

"Jessie, calm down. We'll find her."

Jessie was clutching the jacket to her chest. "I'm in so much trouble."

"I could make flyers and we could put them around the park," Veronica said.

Hilton and Jessie turned to look at her in disbelief.

"I'll make a copy of her picture and we'll leave contact numbers. She's bound to show up. It'll work," Veronica said confidently. She gently touched Jessie's shoulder. Jessie looked at her as if she was a guardian angel.

Dave had come out of the control room. He leaned over and whispered to Hilton, "Dude, I think you've been replaced."

"I see that. It must have been really meaningful."

"Chicks are like that. Rip your heart out and serve it like a shish kabob. It's so wrong. By the way, Anne wants to know why a grownup has a teddy bear."

Hilton smirked. "Tell her it's a long story."

"But I don't have a picture of the bear," Jessie said mournfully.

"Let me see the jacket," Veronica commanded.

Jessie gingerly handed it over.

Veronica looked at the label of the jacket. "Just as I suspected."

"What?" Jessie asked.

"It's a Vermont Teddy Bear. Hilton, pull up their Web site and download a picture."

"Yes, ma'am." Hilton could see Anne pacing and listening or pretending to be listening to a caller and watching the clock for the end of the show. She clearly wanted out.

They went back into the control room and crowded around Hilton's computer desk.

"You're brilliant," Jessie told Veronica. Hilton could see she was filled with admiration.

"God, this is making me sick," Dave said.

"Exactly, pass the barf bag," Hilton said. She pulled up the Web site and began searching for the bear.

"Dudes, if we know the Web site can't you just order another bear?" he said.

"We can't. The bear had identifying characteristics," Jessie said, sitting on the corner of Hilton's desk.

"Like what?" Dave asked.

Lillian was staring intently at Jessie, who smiled and waved at her. "Like this sterling silver locket thing she has hanging around her neck," Jessie replied.

"Dude, the bear has jewelry," Dave said incredulously.

Lillian pulled off her headphones. "You look just like my second cousin's dead nephew," she said, pointing at Jessie.

"Great," Jessie said, looking to Hilton for guidance. Hilton shrugged. "How'd he die?" she asked.

Hilton stifled a laugh as Dave gave Jessie the don't-go-there look. Jessie, of course, didn't get it.

"Well, you see, one year down on the river . . ." Lillian started.

"Lillian, the show's almost over and you've got to clear the lines. Maybe you can tell us the story later," Dave suggested.

"Right, but you are the spitting image of him, poor little fellah." She put her headphones back on and got to work.

Hilton had located and printed off a picture of Amelia Bearhart.

"Okay, Jessie, come with me." Veronica snatched the copy from Hilton. "We'll get the flyers going so right after the show we can canvas the area. Time is of the essence. I think we can discount Lillian due to her age, but the rest of us, including Dave, could cover a lot of ground."

Dave gave her a look. "Gee, it's a good thing I didn't have plans."

Over her shoulder Veronica said, "You might think about inviting the mail harlot to make your community service more palatable."

"It'll look good for your new girlfriend. It'll show your sensitive side," Hilton added.

"I guess you're right," Dave replied. He didn't look completely convinced.

Anne came flying out of the booth. "My goodness, I thought the show would never end. Dave, did you have to leave me hanging out there so long? Good God! How about some extra commercials or something? I'm sick of stupid stories and I have to pee like a racehorse. Hilton, come with me and fill me in."

Hilton got up and was about to follow Anne when Lillian nearly plowed her over.

"Dude, be careful. I got between her and her cigarette break once and got cold-cocked. She's built like a Mack truck."

"I'll remember that next time," Hilton said. She followed Anne into the restroom and sat on the vanity while Anne took care of her bodily needs.

"I don't remember anything in my contract that stated I needed a gallon-sized bladder."

"It's all the coffee you drink. Coffee is a diuretic."

"Oh, well, that's not happening anytime soon. I love coffee."

"Perhaps we could put in a requisition for a portable toilet in the booth."

Anne laughed. "I could just see Veronica denying the purchase order as an unnecessary expense. Now, what's going on with your friend and Veronica. I swear it looked like love at first sight."

It was Hilton's turn to laugh. "No, say it isn't so. Actually, we have a big household problem."

"Can I help?" Anne said. She washed her hands.

"Not unless you're good with a staple gun."

"I've never actually used one but I can't imagine they're that difficult. What is Jessie so upset about?"

"She lost Amelia Bearhart at the park and she wanted to use Shannon as a tracker dog."

"I see. Can I ask a personal question?"

"Sure." Hilton hopped down from the vanity.

"What's a grown-up woman doing with a teddy bear? I mean, isn't she a little old for toys?"

"It's not hers."

"Oh, the plot thickens."

"It belongs to our other roommate Liz's girlfriend. Jessie was bear-sitting while they went out for lunch. I think it's part of Liz's plan to get Melissa to loosen her hold on the bear."

"But why does she have the bear?"

"She was traumatized when her first lover—and from the sounds of it, her only girlfriend—left her. She gave her the bear as a surrogate, I suppose. She takes it with her everywhere."

"So Jessie is in deep shit if we don't find the bear."

"We need to mobilize—flyers everywhere—and hopefully the bear will be returned to its rightful owner."

There was a knock on the door. "Dudes, Veronica says we've got to move it, like time is of the essence or some shit," Dave said.

"Veronica is kind of a control freak," Hilton said.

"You just noticed that?"

Hilton pinched her arm. "Gran said you should always assume people are good . . ."

"Until they screw you," Anne finished.

"Yeah, and then she said you can let the big guns out."

"I would have liked her," Anne said, opening the door for Hilton.

"What on earth were you two doing in there for so long?" Veronica said. Her arms were full of flyers that she immediately thrust at Hilton. "We've got to get moving if we're to find the bear and save Jessie from certain torture."

"Hilton has irritable bowel syndrome. Cut her some slack."

Hilton's jaw dropped and she gaped at Anne.

Anne laughed and then gave her a shove. "Chop chop. We're behind schedule and we haven't even begun."

"I'm going to get you for that," Hilton said. "I can't believe you said that."

"I amaze myself sometimes. Now, let's go find the bear."

They headed across town to Lincoln Park. Veronica, as she was known to do, coordinated the troops and sent everyone off. Veronica and Jessie headed west. Dave and his girlfriend, Gwin, headed south while Hilton, Anne and Shannon were sent off to the eastern end. Shannon rebelled and went off to sit under a big sugar maple tree whose leaves were still holding but had turned bright yellow.

"All right, but no wandering," Hilton told her.

"I wish I had a camera," Anne said. She pointed to the yellow tree with the white dog under a perfect blue sky. It would make a great screen saver."

"You want a picture?"

"Yes."

Hilton rummaged around in her backpack and pulled out her digital camera. She pointed it at Anne and took a photo.

"You truly are a gear queen. But I don't want a picture of me."

"I know. But I do. It's payment." Hilton pointed the camera at Shannon and took another photo. Shannon, who had had hundreds of pictures taken of her, seemed to almost pose. Hilton had exactly one photo of her father and two of her mother. That was why she had purchased the camera, so that her life would stop passing her by with nothing to document the passing of time. She showed the picture to Anne. "Is that what you want?"

"That's perfect. Thank you."

Veronica came marching over.

"Oh, we're in trouble now," Anne said.

"Watch this," Hilton said. She took another photo.

"You two are supposed to be getting flyers up." Veronica seemed not to notice that her control-freak behavior had just been photo-documented.

"All right, we're going," Hilton said. She stuffed the camera back in her bag.

"Start twelve blocks away and then start moving back toward the park," Veronica instructed.

When Veronica was out of earshot, Anne asked, "What are you going to do with that photo?"

"Put it on the Web site with an applicable caption."

Anne laughed. "You're almost as bad as I am."

They left Shannon resting under the tree and trudged off three blocks. Anne pointed out various architectural styles of the old houses they passed. Hilton was still stewing about what a horrible control freak Veronica was. This was classic displacement, she knew. A therapist would tell her that she was angry with Jessie for losing the bear, and she was worried about Liz losing her chance at love because of the lost bear. Veronica was only trying to help.

"Okay, let's start here." Her mood was improving now that she'd done some processing. She unlocked and loaded the staple gun as Anne looked on.

"You know, power tools and tools in general have always fascinated me, but they kind of make me nervous at the same time."

Hilton laughed. "You do have to be careful but staple guns are pretty harmless."

"They do look pretty rudimentary," Anne said as she handed Hilton a flyer.

They hit every telephone pole they could find for ten blocks.

"Maybe I should try the staple gun," Anne suggested.

"Did Gerald do everything?" Hilton asked, wondering what Anne's ex-husband looked like.

"Yes. I was always the assistant."

"Well, then it's high time you tried your hand at it." Hilton put the safety latch on the gun and handed it to her. "When you're ready, pull this off and then push down on the lever."

Anne lined up the flyer and then perfectly stapled it. She jumped a little as the gun went off but that was all.

"See, that was awesome. Come on, let's try some more."

"I did jump a little."

"I hardly noticed."

Anne smiled at her. They hit a few more poles until they stood at the last one at the edge of the park. Shannon was still sleeping under the tree. Anne was poised to fire when she stopped. "Oh, my God, will you look at that."

"What?" Then Hilton saw. Veronica was rubbing Jessie's shoulders as she sat on one of the park benches. They were engrossed in discussion. She wondered where Dave and his girlfriend had gotten off to.

"What's up with that? It almost has an element of tenderness," Anne said.

"I think it's love at first sight."

"No way!" Anne was behind her at the telephone pole and cocking the staple gun again.

"Who would have thought," Hilton said, bemused with the idea. She could just imagine Jessie, complete with leather outfit, living happily ever after under Veronica's domination.

"Oh, no!" Anne screeched.

Hilton whipped around. She saw Anne's thumb stapled to the pole. "Holy shit. Will it come off?"

"I hope so or we'll have to call the fire department." Anne lifted her thumb off the pole.

"That's a good sign." Then she saw the staple had gone clean through the corner of Anne's thumbnail. "Kind of."

"I might have to cry," Anne said, peering down at it.

"Perfectly understandable."

"I think we need to get this removed."

Hilton whistled for Shannon, who came running, and they hustled over to where Veronica and Jessie were sitting.

"All finished?" Jessie said brightly.

"You could say that. Anne stapled her thumb."

"Ouch! Let me see that." Anne produced the damaged appendage. Veronica peered at it and winced. It was almost a wince of compassion, Hilton thought ruefully.

"I can get that out." Jessie made for her car and came back with an opened pint of Jack Daniels and a screwdriver.

Anne was obviously mortified as Jessie came toward her. "We'll just pop it out. But here, take a few swigs of this first." She handed Anne the bottle.

Anne took two swigs and then took two more. "Oh, now that was a good idea."

Hilton intervened. "Jessie, this isn't the Wild West. We need to take her to the emergency room and have it surgically removed, like in a sterile environment."

Jessie looked crestfallen.

"It was a nice thought, Jessie, but I think Hilton is right. Although, the Jack Daniels makes a great painkiller," Anne said diplomatically. She took another swig.

"You guys find Dave and Gwin and we'll go get this taken care of. Jessie, can you take Shannon with you? And for goodness' sakes don't lose her," Hilton said.

"I won't. Then we can all meet back at the house. There'll be less of a scene if there's a crowd. You know, when Melissa finds out."

"Jessie, you know our house never looks that great." Hilton was envisioning the party days with the liquor bottles and pizza boxes everywhere and the no-longer-stain-resistant living room furniture.

"No, today is different. Well, actually from now on it'll be different."

"Why is that?" Hilton asked.

"The Merry Maids are coming today, and I ordered new furniture. It came this morning. The place looks great. I sent the bill to the accountant. He wasn't real happy about it until I mentioned that as an heiress you shouldn't be living in a biohazard. I told him Nat was gone. Then he seemed all right with the improvements."

Anne looked on wide-eyed and then took another swig. Hilton just laughed. "So you're in charge now."

"Well, yeah. Look, Nat's gone and so are the people who used to trash the house. So I took the liberty to spiff up the place and then . . . I lost the bear."

"It's going to work out. Take everyone home and we'll meet you there."

Anne handed Hilton the car keys. "I don't think I can drive or should drive."

"Are you okay? You're not going into shock, are you?" Hilton studied the hanky that Anne had wrapped around her thumb. It was bloody.

"No, but after all the JD I don't think I should get behind the wheel."

Hilton drove them to Saint John's Hospital. At one o'clock in the afternoon the emergency room was relatively slow. Hilton figured that it was the middle of the day and the middle of the week. Not exactly prime time for auto accidents, stabbings, gunshot wounds or cutting your hand off with a table saw.

As the nurse led them to an examination room forty-five minutes later, she asked, "Are you a relative?"

"Yes, Hilton's my sister and I'm going to need her moral support."

"All right, then. The doctor will be with you shortly."

"That was quick on your part," Hilton whispered.

"Aren't we all brothers and sisters in God's eyes? Is this like a Homoslavia issue?"

"Yes, and one of the big ones. Usually, we lie like you just did but sometimes it doesn't work and then we run into problems."

Anne sat on the exam table and Hilton took the chair. She hated hospitals. It always reminded her of Gran dying and the months she had spent there waiting for death to come.

The doctor came in. "So what do we have here?" He was young with dark hair and dressed in wrinkled green scrubs. He peered down at her thumbnail. "Ouch."

"That's what I said," Anne replied.

"Were you drinking when you did this?" the doctor asked as he prepared a syringe.

"No, that was afterward, but I did turn down an offer to have it plucked out with a screwdriver."

"Good choice. This is going to prick a bit. It's a shot of Novocain just to numb it up."

"I think that's a marvelous idea."

Hilton's cell phone went off. It was Liz frantically yelling, "Tell me those flyers I saw on the way home weren't for our bear."

Hilton took a deep breath. "Liz, it's all right. Jessie is on her way home and I'll be there as soon as we get the staple removed from Anne's thumb."

"Oh, my, is she all right?"

Hilton looked over at Anne, who smiled at her weakly. "Not exactly, but she's got balls."

Hilton turned away when the doctor took out a pair of what looked like pliers and prepared to yank. She took another deep breath.

"Are you all right?" Liz asked.

"I'm not good at this kind of stuff."

"She lost the bear, right?"

"Yes, at the park. We put up flyers everywhere around there. Liz, we'll find the bear. Get out the good brandy and a box of Excaliber cigars and start taking her mind off the bear."

"Why brandy and cigars?"

"It artificially induces dopamine into the system. It makes you feel better."

"I didn't know that."

"Neither did I until I read it in a magazine in the waiting room."

"Hilton?"

"Yes."

"Is Melissa going to hate me?"

"No, she's going to be extremely angry with Jessie. You're going to be her shoulder to cry on, her port in the storm, her staff of moral support . . ."

"Stop. One more cliché and I'll puke."

"Sorry. We'll be home soon." Hilton looked over at Anne, who was having her thumb bandaged up.

"Hilton, what happened to the house?"

"Ask Jessie."

Chapter Eight

Hilton and Anne finally got to the house about five-thirty. They had to stop and get gauze, tape and Anne's prescription for antibiotics filled. Hilton guided them through the back door knowing that the living room was most likely quite busy. Veronica was in the kitchen making a cheese and cracker platter that looked like something straight out of Martha Stewart's magazine. Hilton noticed she'd changed from her office attire to tight black pants and a green and blue paisley ruffled blouse. Her long brown hair hung down her back and swirled around her firm breasts. She was actually beautiful in that haute couture way, Hilton thought. Veronica looked up from her work. "How's the thumb?"

Anne held it up. "The doctor says I'll get to keep the thumb and lose the nail. I can handle that. I've got to keep in wrapped and in this splint for a few days to protect it."

Hilton peeked around the corner into the living room, where she could hear Melissa crying. Liz was sitting next to her, holding her hand and looking empathetic. Jessie was prostrate before her, sitting crouched on the floor, most likely promising things she couldn't deliver. This was only the second time she'd seen Melissa. The night at the party she'd only noticed that she was petite and blond. Now Hilton took a harder look. Melissa had a pretty face with a slightly upturned nose and dark brown eyes. She looked exactly like the Barbie doll's friend Skipper. It was a pity that losing the bear was probably going to remove her from their lives.

Jessie got up and came in the kitchen. She handed Anne a cigar and a brandy, which had been sitting on the counter. "It's not going over well," she said.

"Give her a minute," Hilton said hopefully. She noticed that Jessie had also changed. She was wearing jeans and a tight white T-shirt that showed off her well-defined shoulders and firm abdomen. She picked up one of the radishes off the tray Veronica was preparing. It looked like a tiny red chicken complete with wings and a little beak. "I've never actually known anyone who could do that," she said, pointing at the radishes.

Veronica smiled. "It's quite simple actually. When I'm nervous I do things like this."

"You're so thoughtful," Jessie said as she touched Veronica's shoulder.

"I don't want to be part of the problem. I want to help solve it."

Anne was in the process of lighting her cigar and started to choke. At first, Hilton though she was being facetious about Veronica's comment but then concluded that Anne had no idea what she was doing. Melissa and Liz came into the room.

"I did the same thing," Melissa said. She smiled weakly and Liz squeezed her hand.

"The guys make it look so easy," Anne said, gesturing with the cigar.

"You have to suck slowly and hold the smoke in your mouth and then exhale," Jessie said. She lit her own with absolute finesse.

"I'll try it again if you will," Anne said to Melissa.

"Okay," Melissa said. She took a cigar from the box on the kitchen counter.

Both she and Anne sucked slowly and didn't inhale this time, and both executed a near-perfect display of cigar smoking.

"Awesome," Jessie said.

Hilton took this time to sneak into the living room and check out the new stuff. The mangy cloth sofa had been replaced with a chic brown leather one with a matching chair and ottoman. A flat-screen television replaced the old set. One wall of the living room now housed a cherry wood entertainment center complete with a state-of-the-art stereo system. The wood floor had been scrubbed clean and almost looked shiny, and a beautiful red rug with strategically placed different colored geometric circles was placed in the middle of the room.

"It's Peruvian," Jessie said. "But it was on sale. It's handwoven and helps the economy of the native people. Something about an art co-op thing. I don't know. I just thought it was a cool rug."

"Nice, Jessie. I had no idea you had such good taste," Hilton said.

"I have taste, just no cash to go with it. You really don't mind?"

"No. I have cash and no taste. Maybe you could fix up the place." Hilton gave her a hug. "Thanks, Jessie." She was beginning to feel better about Nat being gone. "Maybe we should paint too," she mused, staring at the dingy white walls. The ceiling in the living room had a water stain from a plumbing problem upstairs.

"And fix the plumbing," Jessie suggested.

"Now that no one will sleep with the plumber," Hilton replied.

"How about a new fridge?" Liz said as she came into the room followed by Melissa, Anne and Veronica.

"One that doesn't leak," Hilton replied.

"Exactly. No more bailing out the produce crisper," Liz said. She flounced down on the couch and Melissa snuggled up next to her.

"What a concept," Hilton said.

"Are you feeling better about the changes in your life?" Liz asked her.

Hilton took a sip of her brandy, surveyed the room again and nodded. "I do believe I am. If we change some things around I might actually forget about her."

Jessie gave her a look that said, "Not in this lifetime."

"I can dream," Hilton said.

"Hilton's girlfriend dumped her for this biker chick," Jessie explained to the others. "I mean, the chick is hot but she doesn't hold a candle to Hilton."

"Jessie!" Liz reprimanded.

"I'm only telling it like it is," Jessie said. She sat down cross-legged on the rug. Anne took the chair and Hilton sat down next to Melissa on the couch. Veronica sat primly on the ottoman.

"Hilton, I'm so sorry. I know just how you must feel," Melissa said. She patted Hilton's thigh sympathetically.

In that moment Hilton knew Melissa would be all right and that she was the best thing that ever could have happened to Liz. "Thanks, Melissa."

"You're right, though, if you change things it reminds you less," Melissa said. She took Liz's hand and smiled at her benevolently. "Liz is helping me forget."

"Oh, hey, Hilton, I forgot to show you the best part," Jessie said as she jumped up. She flipped on the stereo. "I got us XM satellite radio and get this, it's got a salsa station." She found the station and grabbed Veronica.

Veronica, Hilton, Jessie and Liz knew how to dance.

"Why it that?" Anne asked as the four of them danced together.

"Jessie dated a salsa instructor for about a month and we all got free lessons," Liz said.

"Who'd you date?" Veronica asked as she and Jessie swayed in perfect time to the music.

"Chichita Alvarez," Jessie said.

"So did I," Veronica said. "She was hot."

"But crazy and possessive," Jessie added.

Anne looked at Hilton inquiringly. "No, we don't all date the same people and yes, I'm going to teach you how," Hilton replied.

Liz took Melissa's hand and led her out on the floor. Jessie turned the music up a notch higher and soon Melissa and Liz were getting it together.

"You know I'm rhythmically impaired," Anne said, following Hilton to an empty area in the corner of the room.

"This is different than freestyle dance. There are prescribed moves," Hilton said. She placed her hands on Anne's hips as professionally as she could muster, but she couldn't help but feel their closeness acutely. She studied Anne's face for a moment.

"Have I ever told you that I have the best time with you?" Anne said.

"Am I really that entertaining?"

"Or are my other friends that boring? Oh, yeah, they're all married with two-point-five children and bitchy."

Hilton laughed. "Come on, let me show you the moves."

After about three songs Anne and Melissa had the rudimentary parts down, not that they'd win a salsa competition but that didn't deter from the level of fun they were all having. Hilton looked over to see Melissa smiling and giggling as Liz moved her around, and Anne was making a pretty good partner. She'd only stepped on Hilton's foot twice and tripped them both once.

"We need margaritas," Veronica said with a laugh.

"Yes!" Jessie replied. They headed off to the kitchen.

They returned shortly with a pitcher of margaritas and the evening was off to a fine start. Hilton knew the lost bear was still in the back of everyone's mind, but music and fun had a lot of mileage on the road to distraction.

Hours later, Hilton and Anne sat on the back porch steps cooling off. The sky was clear and the yard almost looked well-trimmed in the light of the quarter moon. Much of the deciduous flora had shed its summer leaves, giving a false sense of neatness to the landscaping.

"Good God, I bet I burned off five thousand calories, despite the cheese platter, the nachos and the margaritas," Anne said. She lit her cigar. "I think I'm getting the hang of these."

"I think you are, and about the calories, have you ever seen a fat salsa dancer?"

Anne laughed. "Uh, no. Hey, what's that over there?" she said, pointing into the dimness.

"It's the cottage. I think it was the servants' quarters at one time. It's my bedroom now."

"But I thought you slept in the attic."

"What did you think that I slept in the middle of the skate bowl?"

"Is that what that thing is?"

"Yeah, I bought it off this guy for five hundred bucks. We took it apart and then reassembled it in the attic. I love to skateboard but the parks are so crowded with kids who look at you funny now that you're old in their eyes. So I made my own."

"You are the only skateboarder I know that's over twelve."

"See."

"This is a great house." Anne looked up at the third story.

"It needs some work, and now that Nat's gone along with her destructive entourage we can fix it up. You want to see the cottage?"

"Sure."

Shannon was inside sleeping on the bed. She licked Anne's hand and curled up. "Had a long day, girl?" Hilton said.

The cottage looked suspiciously clean. Jessie's Merry Maids must have made a swoop through the cottage as well. All her records were neatly stacked and everything looked dusted. The carpet had definitely been vacuumed.

"This is cute," Anne said. She sat down on the water bed. "Whoa!"

Shannon opened an eye and sighed heavily. She was obviously perturbed.

"Sorry about that. I haven't sat on one of these in forever." Anne looked around the room some more. "Quite the record collection."

"It's another one of my passions."

"Play me something."

"Sure. Do you want a beer?" Hilton opened her dorm fridge and peered inside. There were four Rolling Rocks and one Amstel Light.

"Oh, I don't know about that. I think between my thumb and the margaritas I've got enough going on trying to get home."

"You relinquished the right to drive after your third margarita."

"Are you making me hand over my car keys?" Anne took the beer Hilton handed her.

"I still have them."

"That's right." Anne took a sip of beer.

"You can have the bed and I'll sleep on the floor." Hilton studied her record piles looking for just the right tune.

"Hilton, this bed is enormous. I think the three of us can find room enough to sleep. I promise not to seduce you."

"I didn't mean that." Hilton blushed.

"Let's have a nightcap and call it an evening," Anne said.

"I'll go get a bowl of ice for your hand. Remember, the doctor said you're supposed to ice it to keep the swelling down."

"You know, it's funny he didn't mention margaritas, salsa or cigars. Those activities have done wonders as well."

"You're a terrible patient," Hilton said. She put on a Van Morrison record and went back to the house.

The stereo was turned off and Jessie and Veronica were nowhere in sight. Hilton was poking around in the freezer in search of ice when she heard Liz and Melissa in the hallway.

"I don't think it's such a bad idea," Liz said gently.

"I just think if I remove myself from my normal surroundings I won't think about her," Melissa said.

"I'd love for you to stay. We've got extra linens. We could set you up in my room and I'll sleep on the couch."

There was silence.

"Or we could both sleep in your room," Melissa suggested.

"If you'd like."

Then they were quiet. Hilton smiled. She imagined Liz's face as she tried to mask her fear and desire. Hilton wondered how successful she was.

When she got back to the cottage Anne had fallen asleep. Hilton removed her shoes and pulled the comforter over her. She turned the record player off. Shannon was snoring slightly. Hilton put the bowl of ice on Anne's side of the bed then looked at Anne for a moment. She could almost imagine them doing this all the time. She suppressed the urge to curl up next to her and stroke her cheek and then kiss her softly on the lips. She sighed, thinking, not in this lifetime. It was like the pretend game she played as a child where her mother was alive and her father was nice and they all lived in blissful communion. Her brow wrinkled in consternation and she turned off the light.

Chapter Nine

Hilton was nowhere to be found in the morning when Anne woke up. She leaned over and put her face on Hilton's pillow. It smelled like her. She remembered last night and how pleasant and oddly seductive it was to sleep next to someone you weren't supposed to touch. She lay back on her side of the bed and gazed at the ceiling as the morning light filtered through the curtains. Her thumb was throbbing and she looked at the now melted bowl of ice. The bedside clock read seven.

She tried to stay still for a moment longer before the whirlwind of the day came crashing through her mind. She held out as long as she could. Then she got up and began her frantic search for information. There was no radio, no television and no computer in the cottage. She had to pee so she opted for bathroom time and then she would wander up to the house and get a cup of coffee. Anne wondered if Hilton had left so they wouldn't be forced to wake up together or if something had happened in the house.

Hilton had obviously put out a washcloth, a bar of soap and a toothbrush still in its wrapper, complete with a tiny tube of toothpaste. All appeared to have been lifted from a hotel. Anne smiled, remembering her own college days when anything complimentary came home as future provisions. Something warm and wet licked her ankle. She patted Shannon's head. "Good morning," she said. Shannon sighed heavily and went to lay on the bath mat. She fell back asleep as Anne washed up.

Once tidied she made her way to the house. The now almost constant cloud cover had small breaks in it, but it looked like the day was set for rain. She slipped in the back door and found Hilton getting a tray together.

Hilton looked up and smiled. "You're supposed to still be asleep so I could bring you coffee in bed."

"Really? I could go back."

"You better. We've got time and I did some research for you on opposable thumbs for the show. You know you're going to go there."

"You mean my opening monologue?" Anne queried. She greedily eyed the corner hutch, noticing it contained a laptop and a printer. "May I?"

"Of course," Hilton handed her a stack of Internet documents.

Anne took the stack of papers and leafed through them. "Very good." She hit the home page on the computer to pick up the latest news.

"It's kind of slow today. The Dow is up two points and it's going to rain."

"Like that's news," Anne said. She typed in a couple of keywords until she contented herself with the fact that nothing truly amazing had happened in the last twenty-four hours.

"Shall we go to the cottage?" Hilton asked as she picked up the tray with the carafe, cups, cream and sugar.

"Please. I'm glad it's going to be a comedy show today. I don't feel like doing hard news."

There was giggling in the hallway. Jessie and Veronica appeared in the kitchen wrapped up in each other's arms.

"Veronica?" Anne said, stunned.

"Anne, what are you doing here?" Veronica said, trying to straighten herself out. Her shirt was badly wrinkled and her always perfect hair was disheveled. Anne had never seen her look so flustered.

"I'm having coffee with Hilton and going over some notes for today's show," Anne said. She waved the stack of papers as proof. She winked at Hilton.

"Well, of course. Jessie and I were just on our way out for breakfast." She yanked Jessie's hand. "I'll see you at work."

"Sure, great. Jessie, don't make her late for work," Anne said. She loved to tease Veronica and this morning was going to give her months of ammunition. Veronica had been the radio show's producer for five years. This was as social as the two of them had ever gotten. Anne wasn't certain she liked it. Veronica was a master manipulator and the closer together their lives got the more control she would try to exert.

It was Anne and Hilton's turn to giggle on the way back to the cottage.

"Did you see the look on her face?" Anne said.

"I don't think it even occurred to her that you stayed here as well."

"That's the best part."

Some patches of sun managed to burst forth from the clouds, making the morning seem almost sunny and crisp. The last days of fall were hanging on with a vigor unlike itself. The rains of winter usually had killed it off by now.

When they got to the cottage Shannon was finally awake and wanted to go out. Anne watched as she squatted to pee and then walked the entire perimeter of the yard. She was apparently checking to make sure nothing had infiltrated her domain as she sniffed the ground and rustled about the fallen leaves.

"She does that every morning. That's the comforting thing about dogs, they like to do the same thing everyday. They love routine." Hilton set the tray down on one of the stacks of records.

"If only people found that comforting instead of boring," Anne noted. She took the cup Hilton offered her and then went to sit on the bed. She pulled up the pillows and started to peruse the articles Hilton had pulled off the Internet.

"This is Starbucks house blend and it's kind of stiff. Do you want cream or sugar?" Hilton asked as she poured the coffee.

"A little cream would be good," Anne said.

Hilton handed her a cup. Anne attempted to hold and drink out of her coffee mug with her left hand. The first sip got her neurons jolting and the sickening whirlwind she experienced earlier became the challenge of the day. She was ready to become Seattle's morning talk show host. She wondered if coffee was somehow connected to her personality disorder of wanting to be herself but not wanting herself. Some mornings she didn't want to be Anne Counterman and then she had coffee and was eager to take on whatever crap the world was dishing.

"Do you need a straw?"

"No, I've got it," Anne said. "I'm thinking being ambidextrous might be a good thing. Perhaps I'll start the monologue with that."

"Yeah, then you can move into the story of dolphins spontaneously sprouting thumbs and feeling suicidal at their newfound humanity." Hilton sat down next to her and the bed began to sway.

"And the cats and dogs getting thumb implants and what they'd be capable of," Anne said holding her coffee tightly and waiting for the waterbed to stop moving. "That almost frightens me."

"Shannon would probably want to drive a car or something," Hilton said. She took a sip of coffee.

Anne finished hers. "Okay, I'd better get going. Lord only knows how long it'll take me to get dressed."

"Call me if you need help."

Shannon had come back in. Anne patted her on the head distractedly. "I had a really nice time last night. I mean, it was a lot of fun."

"So did I." Hilton got up and gave her a quick hug.

Anne tried not to blush and then left. Once outside she thought she might be having a hot flash. She couldn't possibly being going through menopause. She knew what it was, but standing outside Hilton's cottage feeling dumbstruck was not the place to analyze her feeling. She got in her car and called Gerald. "Are you alone?"

"Why?" he asked.

"Because I need to talk to you right now." She didn't want her need to be so apparent but her voice cracked and he no doubt knew she was scared.

"Yes, Philip went in early. Why don't you come over and we'll talk."

"I'll be there in ten." She started the car and threw it into drive, glad that it was her left thumb and not her right that was impaired.

"Don't get on the expressway," Gerald advised. "Traffic."

"I'm not stupid," she said testily.

"Anne, whatever this is we can work it out, okay?"

"Yes, 'bye." She clicked off and mentally made a quick map of the best side streets to take to get to his house. She didn't know what exactly she wanted to say to him, but she needed his calming influence and rational way of looking at a situation. He could break down any crisis into manageable pieces that could be systematically dealt with. She missed that about him.

She turned on the radio, hoping for some national news. As she passed through the residential neighborhoods she saw the children dressed up in their Halloween costumes going to school. She could hardly believe that Hilton had only been in her life since the middle of September, that Veronica had given her her one-month pin on Columbus Day, and now here it was Halloween already. Could she have fallen in love in six weeks? Was it a symptom of lust? She hadn't been intimate with anyone in the year since she'd divorced Gerald. She was not a hot-to-trot kind of woman. It must be love. Gerald would know how to sort out this muddle. She turned her attention to the news.

Ten minutes later she arrived at the tasteful yellow and white bungalow that Gerald shared with Philip. He was trying to do his tie and it wasn't going well. "I hate when he leaves early," he said as he let her in. He had on a starched white shirt with his good navy suit. Must be a big day at the office, some marketing proposal most likely, she thought.

"I'd offer to help but I'm kind of out of commission," Anne said, holding up her bandaged thumb.

"What happened?"

"Minor accident with a staple gun."

"Ouch. How did you do that?" he asked.

"Volunteer work," she replied, tucking her hands behind her. She wasn't here to talk about her thumb.

"So what's on your mind?" he asked.

"I want to know how you knew you were in love with Philip?" She paced across the living room. It was already after eight and she was going to be late, but she needed to know. She wandered over to the fireplace mantel and picked up a small carved wooden knick-knack. It was an old habit of hers and she knew Gerald would see right through it. She was trying to be nonchalant and avoid his gaze.

"Anne, what is this really about?"

She picked up a silver-framed picture of her and Gerald on their wedding day. She had that beautiful yet chic white dress on and he looked smart in his gray tux. His dark hair was longer then and he'd somehow tamed his cowlick that day. With his chiseled good looks, he could have been a Calvin Klein model. His blue eyes seemed to sparkle with love and they both looked happy. "He lets you keep that?" She looked at him, puzzled.

"Philip understands that you are an important part of my life. So tell me what's going on." He glanced at his Rolex.

"There's this person who I think I have feelings for and this is all new for me, so I wanted to know how you know when you're truly in love and it's not just, you know, nether region stuff."

"Don't you remember?" he teased.

"With you it was different."

"Why?"

"It seemed I knew you forever, and there wasn't a time when I didn't love you," she said. She took another look at the photograph

114

and then set it back down. She attempted to stick her hands in her pockets and then remembered her thumb, which was still throbbing.

"Let me get us a cup of coffee and we'll talk," he said.

"Please."

He returned with a stainless steel carafe and two cups and set them on the coffee table. Anne smiled, remembering that he had always made a first pot of coffee and then a second, which he put in a carafe in case he wanted more later. He was such a planner. She never did anything just in case.

"Okay, segment one, how do you feel when you're away from this person?"

"Like I can't wait to see them again."

Gerald sat on the couch and patted the seat next to him. "Come, sit."

Anne obeyed. The couch was upholstered in a tasteful sage brocade and went perfectly with the light oak furniture.

"That's a good sign. And what happens when you're together?"

"I have the best time and when it's over all I can think about is when we'll be together again." Anne looked over at him. "It's how I used feel with you." She blushed. All these sensations came flooding over her. It was like a micro-movie of her life, past and present. Falling in love with Gerald, getting mushy inside just watching him walk across the room when they were first going out. And now with Hilton, wanting to touch her bare shoulder this morning as she sat next to her on the bed, her blond hair still messy from sleep. How beautiful she looked dressed in a tank top and flannel pajama bottoms—vulnerable and kind.

"Okay, I'd say you're in love."

"Now, the other side of it is whether they're in love with me. Maybe I'm the only one having this feeling. This is all very confusing." She took a sip of coffee, hoping it would bring her back to normal. She didn't like being this out of control.

"I have an idea. Why don't you bring them over for dinner on your birthday? Philip is chomping at the bit to get me to ask you.

He really wants you to like him. What happened wasn't his fault. It was all about me."

"I think I know that now."

"You know, Anne, maybe we were both pinch hitters in the wrong ballpark."

"How did you know?"

"It's the pronoun game. It's a dead giveaway. What's her name?"

"Hilton."

"Bring Hilton for dinner. In four weeks Philip will have time to plan the dinner of all dinners and you'll know more by then."

"I can hardly think about my birthday yet. We still have to get through Thanksgiving. I can hardly wait. My mother will ask endless questions about you and my father will give me clandestine looks of pity and then finally I'll get to go home feeling a worthless failure."

"You could bring Hilton," he suggested.

She laughed nervously. "I don't think I'm ready for that yet." The image of introducing Hilton to her mother gave her instant heart palpitations. "But I am going to a Halloween party tonight at her place."

He arched an eyebrow then he took her hand. "If you're going to go there, don't hide."

She studied his face for a moment. The gravity of the choices he had had to make came crashing down on her. "It was hard, wasn't it?"

"Very. But it was all worth it. I am who I was truly meant to be and I love Philip very much."

"Okay, I'd better go," Anne said, glancing at her watch.

"Any more questions, feel free." He gave her a hug at the door. "Anne, I never regretted the time we had together."

She stared at him for a moment. "Neither did I."

When Anne got to work everyone was in a panic. The show was to start in twenty minutes. She usually arrived an hour and a half before airtime to do research and get stoked for the two hours ahead.

"Dude, I was almost going to get a 'Best of' show going," Dave said. His usually messy hair was messier than usual. He'd obviously been running his fingers through it in nervous anticipation. In the four years they'd worked together, Anne had pretty much figured out all his stress indicators.

"Here's more notes," Hilton said, handing her a folder and a cup of coffee. "I thought you might need this. Are you okay?"

"I'm fine," Anne said breezily. "It's just a little more difficult getting showered and dressed when you're missing a thumb." She smiled. It was true, but she neglected to mention that she had stopped at Gerald's house on the way home. Sometimes when she looked at Hilton she wasn't certain what she read there. Was it sisterly concern or something more?

"You should have called me. I would've come to help." Hilton reached over and straightened out Anne's shirt collar.

"Thank you." Anne smiled at her, thinking that her look had something more in it.

"Ten minutes, dude," Dave said. He tapped on Lillian's desk. Sometimes Lillian had a power nap before the show. Today was one of those days. She sat straight up, gave a little grunt and slapped her headphones on. Anne adored her. Everyone else at the station thought she was nuts for having a deaf call screener. If they only knew how absolutely entertaining she was.

"Must have stayed late at Bingo last night," Dave said to Anne.

"What's the topic?" Lillian screamed.

"Thumbs," Hilton said.

"Bums, I've known a few in my day. My cousin Mildred married one. He was a cheating lying S.O.B. until the day he died. They think Mildred may have been instrumental in his untimely death. His own tractor ran him over, three times." Lillian chuckled.

Anne glanced at Hilton. She didn't know if she could pull this off.

"It'll be fine. We'll get her straightened out. Just go in there and do your stuff," Hilton said. She sat down at her computer and got the Web cam up and running.

Anne went in the booth and glanced at her notes. She didn't

like winging it. She was kind of like Shannon. She preferred routine days. This wasn't one of them and her mind and body noted the stress. She pulled a packet of Advil Liquid Gels she'd gotten at the convenience store and popped two. Her thumb was killing her. She glanced at the clock. Dave put on the intro tune, followed by top-of-the-hour weather and news. Anne's monologue would follow. She put her headphones on, shut her eyes and took a deep breath. When she opened them she felt centered. She began her monologue.

After thirty minutes of airtime they took a break for station identification, news and weather, followed by commercials. Anne was in the control room watching the playback of the video. Ed, the program director, came into the control room wiping his eyes. "My God, woman, that's the funniest show yet. I'm half tempted to make the staff tape down their thumbs and see how we all get through the day." He winked at Hilton. "You two need to hang out more often. Anne will get herself in the running for the Marconi Award. Carry on."

Anne smiled and gave Hilton a high five with her good hand.

Just then Veronica came flying in. "I have the best news."

"I won the Marconi already?" Anne asked. The Marconi Award was given out each year for best host, best program and a variety of other radio show stuff. It was the equivalent of the Emmys for television. Anne had been in the running a couple of times but had yet to win.

"What?" Veronica asked with a frown.

Hilton and Dave smirked. Veronica put her hand on her hip and pursed her lips. Then she said, "I've located the bear."

Hilton swiveled around in her chair. The expression on her face was one of pure astonishment. "What?"

"Amelia Bearhart has been located. The woman and her child will be bringing the bear in after the show. I've already called Jessie. She's going to locate Liz and Melissa. We shall regroup here for the return of the beloved bear."

"Gee, could we be any more dramatic," Dave grumbled.

"We could if it means mail girl with the fake breasts comes up to see what our hard work produced. I'm thinking a lot of mileage for you, boyfriend," Veronica said snidely.

"Shit! You're right. I'll call down and give her the heads-up. She did put up a lot of flyers yesterday," Dave said, his eyes glossing over. He gave Veronica a big smile.

Veronica hesitated and then smiled back. "You're welcome, Dave."

Dave nearly fell off his chair.

Anne laughed. "Just think, in a mere hour and a half the world will be restored to its rightful self."

Anne watched as Veronica in her tight black skirt and red blazer exited the control room. She noticed her disheveled hair of earlier was now tightly wound up in a neat bun. She was her old self. Anne inwardly sighed. Too many changes too soon made her nervous. Dave leaned back in his chair and said, "I've worked here for four years and Veronica has never smiled at me."

"She got laid last night," Hilton replied.

"That'll do it."

Anne and Hilton laughed. She left for her booth. This time when she put her headphones on she felt better. The rest of the show would be easy.

Chapter Ten

Jessie and Liz arrived first. Their morning classes were over and Jessie had the day off from the gym. Liz's job at the computer lab didn't start until three. Melissa had to take a late lunch break but she was scheduled to show any minute. The bear and her entourage had yet to arrive. Jessie was cooing over Veronica, and Liz was inquiring into the status of Anne's thumb.

"It doesn't hurt as much," Anne replied.

"Dude, I'm so glad you got the bear back," Dave told Jessie she sat on the corner of Hilton's desk in the control room.

"She's lucky because if Amelia didn't show I would've taken a glue gun and sealed her vagina shut permanently," Hilton said sweetly.

Anne looked at Hilton, clearly shocked. She was standing next to Hilton viewing the last playback of the show.

"It's the part below the waist that gets her in trouble," Hilton said. "I'm just looking out for the rest of the world."

Dave got a funny look on his face and Jessie instinctively

grabbed her crotch. "Dude, I don't even have one but that sounds painful."

"You nearly ruined my life," Liz piped in. She was sitting next to Lillian, who was telling a story about her second cousin's nephew who looked just like Jessie.

"I'm so sorry," Jessie said. She actually looked remorseful, Hilton thought.

Hilton added the final touches to the Web site for the day's broadcast. The people who listened to the stream on the Internet were adamant about getting all the details, and they called the station if they weren't satisfied. She added the Halloween graphics Anne had decided on and typed a public service announcement warning everyone to be careful. It was funny how things, through a series of painful convolutions, worked their way out. She wondered if her life would ever find that peaceful sort of resolution.

They were all still talking but had moved into the reception area of the studio. Lillian had finished her story and was off for a Pall Mall. Dave was showing his girlfriend, the mail girl Gwin, the basic features of his D-800 control board. Hilton figured he planned on showing her a lot more later on. Melissa arrived, followed shortly by a woman and her small child.

"Hello, I'm Sarah Carthart and this is my daughter, Tiger Lily."

"Nice to meet you," everyone said in near unison.

"This is Melissa," Liz said.

"Oh, yes, the lost bear's owner," Sarah Carthart said.

Hilton thought the woman looked like a younger version of Sigourney Weaver. The child must have been adopted; she appeared to be Chinese. About two, she was small and had long black hair and was clutching the bear to her chest. This had the potential to be heartbreaking. Hilton wished she could run out and buy the little girl every bear in Seattle just so she wouldn't have to face this loss. The only problem with that was that this bear was the only one she wanted.

Jessie leaned down so she was eye-to-eye with the little girl. "Hi, I'm Jessie. I was the one who lost the bear."

Tiger Lily nodded and held the bear tighter.

"She thought the bear was abandoned so she wanted to take it home and keep it safe," Sarah explained.

"I was helping someone get their dog and when I came back Amelia was gone," Jessie told her.

Hilton was watching Melissa, who didn't appear to be paying any attention to Jessie but rather was staring at Tiger Lily.

Tiger Lily spoke up in toddler English, "I lost once, very scared. My new mom Sarah, she find me and made it all better. Bear lost and scared. I save bear."

"Very good, Tiger Lily, now give the lady her bear back," Sarah prodded.

Tiger Lily looked sadly at the bear, kissed its forehead and whispered something in her ear. After a moment she thrust it at Melissa.

Melissa gave Amelia a squeeze and the held the bear up to her ear. "Tiger Lily, Amelia has decided she wants to stay with you. She says you need her more than I do. Is that all right with you?"

Tears welled up in Tiger Lily's eyes and a huge smile crossed her face. "Really? She said that?"

"Yes," Melissa said as she handed her the bear.

Melissa was looking pretty stoic, Hilton thought. Tiger Lily was dancing around the room with her bear while Sarah thanked Melissa profusely. Anne and Hilton both happened to look over at Dave, who was just then dabbing his eyes with the corner of his T-shirt.

"Oh, my God, will you look at him," Anne whispered to her.

"He's sensitive," Hilton whispered back. "And besides, he's scoring major points with his new girlfriend." Gwin was patting his shoulder.

"Boy, we know who's going to wear the trousers in that family."

Hilton laughed. Life was so odd, she thought. How could one silly inanimate stuffed animal affect so many lives in such a positive way? It was downright weird. Hilton took one last look at Amelia Bearhart as she was carried from the room and wondered how many more lives the tiny fuzzball would change. Well, at least she wasn't like those evil little Gremlins in that horror movie Hilton had seen as a child. Amelia was soft and cuddly and probably supplied hours of anxiety-free sleep.

"So I thought I'd pick up some candy for the Halloween party tonight," Anne said. "Want to come with? This is kind of new to me."

"Of course. Kids are so cute," Hilton said, watching out the reception area window as Tiger Lily and her mother made their way to the elevator. The way Sarah Carthart looked at the daughter made Hilton's heart hurt. Her mother had looked at her that way. She still remembered how it felt to be so unconditionally loved. The last time her mother held her hand was on the beach that fateful day. Hilton sighed heavily.

Anne touched her shoulder. "You okay?"

"Yeah. Come on, let's go shopping." They turned around to bid the others goodbye. Jessie was rubbing Veronica's shoulders as she finished up the day's paperwork and Dave was now showing Liz, Melissa, and Gwin more control room wizardry.

"We reconvene at one-thirty, correct?" Veronica said. "We still have to decorate and get the pumpkins carved. I wish I'd had more advanced notice of this soiree, but I think we can still pull it off in grand style."

"You did just meet Jessie yesterday," Anne reminded her.

"I know but some things are meant to be," Veronica said, looking goo-goo-eyed at Jessie.

"I think I'm going to be ill," Anne said.

Hilton gave her a little shove. "Come on, this is good for her. If she's in love she's a lot less of a pain in the ass as a producer."

"You do have a point there," Anne said. They headed for the elevators.

They got back to the house at one-thirty after having made great time at Fred Meyers gathering up a shopping cart full of candy, decorations and six pumpkins. They chose the biggest pumpkin they could find for Veronica. "Let's see the maestro carve a swan or something out of this," Anne said, lugging it to the front porch. She set it next to the bale of straw sitting there. "What the hell?"

"I'm sure Veronica is inside sewing a scarecrow to go with," Hilton said.

Anne screamed, "Ouch!" as the big pumpkin rolled onto her thumb.

"Are you all right?" Hilton asked.

"Yes, I just bumped it."

They got the rest of the stuff out of the car and made trips to the foyer where they stashed it all. Shannon was sniffing the bale of straw and then apparently decided it would make a good bed. She climbed on top of it and resumed her napping. Anne scratched her ears and then followed Hilton into the house where someone was screeching in pain. Hilton could only imagine.

"I have to pee," Anne said, looking around. Hilton pointed to the first-floor toilet that had now officially been repaired. Jessie had dealt with the plumber that morning.

"I'll go see what the ruckus is about," Hilton said. She left the front door cracked so Shannon could come in when she was finished pretending she was a farm dog. She found Jessie leaning over the sink with her hair under the faucet. She was screaming as Liz told her to stay still. "What the hell is going on?"

"Jessie's got corn syrup in her hair and I'm trying to get it out," Liz said.

"How did that happen?" Hilton asked. She looked around the kitchen at the huge bowl of colored popcorn balls, decorated sugar cookies and three boxes filled with what looked like craft supplies.

Jessie pulled her head out of the sink. "I was cleaning up the pan with the corn syrup in it and I got an itch."

"Which she scratched with her sticky hand and what do you know it's stuck in her hair," Liz added.

Hilton chuckled.

"I want to get it out before Veronica comes down. I don't want her to think I'm a dweeb," Jessie said, pulling at the blob of syrup still stuck in her hair.

"Where is Veronica?" Hilton asked.

"She's upstairs in Gran's old sewing room making a skirt for her witch's costume. She wants to be scary when she hands out the candy," Jessie replied.

"She's making a skirt," Hilton said incredulously.

Anne came in the kitchen. "Why do you have a bunch of sheets soaking in black dye in the bathtub?"

"What?" Hilton said.

"Veronica is dyeing them black so we can cut designs in them. You hang them up and the design utilizes inside lights," Liz replied.

"Ouch!" Jessie said as Liz attempted to pull the corn syrup out of her hair.

"What's that?" Anne said, leaning in to take a closer look.

"Corn syrup," Jessie replied.

"You're going to have to cut it out," Anne said.

"Really?" Jessie's eyes got big.

"I could probably do it," Anne said.

"You cut hair?" Hilton asked.

"Well, I do a little trimming on my own."

"I always wondered how your hair looked so perfect all the time," Hilton said.

"It's maintenance," Anne said, touching the bottom of her curly locks. "Come on, let's get this out of Jessie's hair before Martha Stewart on steroids gets wind of it."

"Let's hit the library. She won't look for us there. Liz, you run defense. Do we even have scissors?" Hilton asked. She eyed the craft boxes. "We do now," she said, plucking out a pair of orange-handled scissors.

"I think I'm having a panic attack," Liz said. She sat down at the kitchen table.

"Why?" Jessie asked, still pulling at her hair.

"I'm supposed to be cutting out these designs for the pumpkin carving. Then I've got to find that old black kettle that's some-where in the depths of the garage and get some dry ice. I have to go to work at three and pick Melissa up at six-thirty and get back here to finish helping," Liz said, draping her head in her hands.

"I'll find the pot and get the dry ice. You sit here and cut out the designs. Have a cup of tea and go to work," Hilton instructed.

"And we'll deal with Veronica," Anne piped in.

Hilton led them to the library. For the first time in her life she was embarrassed at the state of the place. It was far more tattered than the living room ever had been. The old brown and gold brocade couch and matching chairs were tattered and the Mexican blankets bought from the flea market to cover up the worn furniture could definitely use a washing. Shannon slept on the couch a lot and it was covered with white fur. The old oak and glass bookcases had held up somewhat, but the books lay in messy stacks as if someone had carelessly rooted through them.

Anne didn't appear to notice. "Jessie, sit on the ottoman and we'll get you all fixed up."

"Hey, Jessie, why don't you work on fixing this room up as well," Hilton suggested.

"Really?" Jessie said. She sat up straight as Anne surveyed her head.

"Yeah, you did a great job on the living room."

"This room has great lines. What with the oak paneling and the big windows it could be a real showplace," Anne said. She clipped out the corn syrup.

"I'll call the accountant and tell him what we're up to," Hilton said.

"Okay, it's going to be shorter," Anne said. "But it's the only way I can even it out."

"Can you take some off the top?" Jessie asked.

"Jessie, she's not a real hair stylist," Hilton said. She sat on the couch. Shannon must have heard them because she came inside and jumped on the couch next to her.

"I think I can do that," Anne said, standing back and then coming in and making a few snips here and there.

"Speaking of haircuts, I know someone who's going to the groomer this week," Hilton said. Shannon barked.

"Is that as bad as going to the vet?" Anne asked. She clipped a little more off the top of Jessie's head.

"Not quite. The groomer is mobile so she comes to the house. Shannon doesn't get as upset and she gets a lot of treats."

"Did you want a little trim?" Anne asked.

"What do you have in mind?" Hilton asked.

"Well, I was thinking about taking off a couple of inches. That would get rid of all your split ends and encourage healthy growth."

"Do it. She did a great job on my hair," Jessie said, admiring her hair in the oval beveled mirror that hung over the fireplace mantel.

Hilton took a handful of hair and studied the ends. It was badly damaged. "All right."

"Come sit on the ottoman." Anne combed out the snarls and then began to cut.

"There you are!" Veronica said as she entered the den.

"Where's Liz?" Hilton asked. Anne was putting the final touches on her trim job.

"She had to go to work."

Hilton glanced down at her Swiss Army watch, thinking sure she did. It was only five after two and her shift didn't start until three.

"You look great!" Jessie said.

"Why, thank you," Veronica said, swirling around to better show off her ensemble.

"I can't believe you just whipped up a skirt," Anne said. She was still seriously studying Hilton's hair.

"Oh, it was easy. I took some old sheets, dyed them black, which takes no time at all and then dried them. Hilton, you really need a new dryer. That thing is archaic. Then I sewed a hem and a waistband. Your grandmother's sewing machine, however, is top of the line. I fed some elastic through the waistband. And there you have it. Wear a long sleeved black sweater, buy an inexpensive witch's hat and off you go."

Hilton felt exposed, like she was on display. She was glad that she had company because being so close to Anne sometimes made her kind of giddy. She swore Anne's cologne sent her endorphins into overdrive.

127

Anne stood back. "I think it's even."

"Thank you," Hilton said. She got up and surveyed herself in the mirror over the fireplace. Her hair did look better.

"Veronica, I seriously think you could give Martha Stewart a run for her money. Your talents are being wasted as a radio show producer."

Veronica was still and quiet for a moment. "Thank you, Anne. You're the first person who has ever really appreciated my home-making talents."

"You do totally rock," Jessie said.

"Well, that's enough about me. Let's get to decorating," Veronica said.

Hilton stifled a groan. Anne touched her hand. "Come on, it'll be fun."

"Yeah, like having your toenails removed."

Later that evening as they all lay around the living room on pil-lows and afghans watching *Tales from the Crypt* on DVD, Hilton thought the afternoon and evening had been more fun than she imagined possible. It was certainly better than last year when the entire evening had been spent doing Ecstasy and finding Nat in the arms of a woman dressed as a belly dancer.

This year was wholesome in comparison. Veronica and Anne handed out candy. The carved pumpkins turned out to be amazingly creative. The black cauldron spewing froth and the decorations in the windows made the old Victorian house look downright scary. Veronica had allowed them to order takeout Chinese instead of whipping up something herself, so after the trick-or-treaters were gone they had time to relax. Hilton lay next to Anne on a blanket. They propped up pillows against the couch and covered up with a throw. The night was chilly. Hilton felt Anne's thigh next to hers and she couldn't help thinking if this was her life she would die happy.

Chapter Eleven

The following Saturday Hilton, Jessie and Liz sat on the sand at the beach staring at the small shrine Hilton had built for the occasion. She lit three votive candles, one for the past, one for the present and one for the future. She put a picture of her mother in the middle of them and then lay a giant sunflower at its base. Sunflowers were her mother's favorite flower. The picture was Hilton's favorite. It was one of her mother as a young woman perched on a bicycle, her legs spread wide and a girlish grin on her face.

Hilton lay back on the old quilt and stared up at the sky. The November gloom was settling in. The city would be monochromatic for the next few months ahead. Maybe this year she'd really go to Mexico and get some sun like she promised herself every year. It always seemed something would come up or she'd find an excuse not to go. She imagined herself lying on the beach, wearing only a sarong. Every part of her would be brown and she'd buy a bunch of cheap silver bracelets because they always looked good against tanned skin. She wondered if her mother ever felt like running away to somewhere warm and simple, somewhere away from Percy.

"Hilton?" Jessie said, breaking Hilton's ruminations.

"Yes." She opened her eyes and sat up.

"How come he always sits up there in his big fat limo and never talks to you?"

Jessie was referring to her father, Percy Withers, who sat in the back of his black limo in the parking lot of the beach each year on this day. It was the only time she saw him, or rather, felt his presence. She couldn't actually see him behind the tinted windows of the backseat, but his driver always waved so she'd know it was Percy. His driver seemed a decent man. Sometimes he'd get out of the limo and have a cigarette. Percy would stay as long as she did. She would leave with her friends and the limo would drive off.

"There's a few reasons, I think." She shrugged. "Guilt, shame and greed."

"Guilt for letting your mom die, shame because he didn't save her, but I don't get the third one," Jessie said, eyeing the limo. Percy's driver was leaning on the side of the limo smoking. He was dressed in a black suit with a white shirt.

"Greed can be something more than money. He wants it all. He wants her memory, her death, her child, and he wants to suck the life out of all of them," Hilton replied.

Liz took Hilton's hand and squeezed it gently. "Did you invite Anne?"

"Yes."

"I thought you would," Liz said.

"How did you know?"

"Because she's close to you now. It's all right, Hilton. Our little family could stand some expansion."

Hilton smiled.

Just then Anne came down the path to the beach that overlooked Puget Sound. She was carrying a bag from Pike's Street

Market. "I know it's November and kind of chilly but I brought us a little picnic," she said. She saw the shrine. "It's beautiful, Hilton. Your mother must have been a special woman."

"It's our way of remembering her," Hilton replied.

Anne put the bag down. Jessie started pawing around in it. "Wine, cheese, a baguette and grapes, red and green. Yum. How come we never thought of that?"

Liz gave her one of her "You're such a swine" looks.

"Well, it seems like such a good idea," Jessie said. "That's all I meant."

"Come see the shrine up close," Hilton said as she took Anne's hand. It wasn't until they'd taken a few steps that Hilton realized what she'd done. It felt good. It felt natural and Anne didn't appear to think it was weird so Hilton tried to relax.

"That's her?" Anne asked, pointing to the picture.

"Yes, when she was about my age."

"You look a lot like her. She was very pretty." Anne squatted down next to the shrine.

"Thank you for coming. I know it's kind of sad and weird."

"It's all right, Hilton. Really. I'm just glad you wanted me to be a part of it." Anne stood and touched Hilton's cheek.

Hilton closed her eyes and basked for a moment. She knew if Jessie saw this her conjectures would all be proven correct. Hilton knew she was right, only she wasn't ready to let her feelings surface or discuss them with anyone, including Anne.

Anne broke her reverie. "What's with the limo?"

"It's Percy."

"I didn't know you two talked."

"We don't. He just comes and sits in the limo each year."

"What! He gets this close to you and never says a word? That's not right. Mind if I go have a word with him?"

"What would you say?"

"I'm going to tell him what a schmuck he is, that he has an incredible daughter and he might want to get to know her before it's too late."

"Feel free. Beware of the cold fish." Hilton couldn't decide if she was scared or amused by Anne's sudden defense of her.

Anne went tromping up to the parking lot.

"Where's she going?" Liz asked in a panic.

"She's going to tell Percy that he's a schmuck for hiding out in the limo." Hilton chuckled to herself, thinking that anyone who could make Percy feel uncomfortable scored big points in her world.

"Awesome," Jessie said.

Hilton sat down on the quilt.

"Is that such a good idea?" Liz asked tentatively.

"I can't see how it can possibly hurt." Hilton stared out at the surf as it came rolling in. She heard the distinct rumble of a Harley as it came up the road. She lay down and rolled on her side, propping herself up on one elbow and facing Liz. "Tell me it's not her."

"It's not her."

Hilton rolled onto her back and closed her eyes, letting out a sigh of relief. She really didn't want to see Nat right now.

"Hilton?" Liz said. "I lied. Just be polite. She won't stay long. She doesn't have that kind of attention span."

Hilton sat up. Shannon, who'd been chasing gulls on the beach, came roaring back. She barked at Nat, who stuck her hands in her pockets and almost looked shy.

"Hey," Hilton said.

"I just thought I'd stop by, and you know, pay my respects."

"That's nice, Nat," Liz said diplomatically.

"Percy here?" Nat glanced up at the limo.

"Same as always," Hilton replied. Anne was standing with her back to the beach and talking with Percy.

"How's Emily?" Nat asked.

"She's great!" Jessie interjected. "They hang out all the time."

"Cool. Well, I've go to go. Sherry's waiting."

"Sure," Hilton said. She watched her walk up the hill. She waited for her heart to explode and bleed all over the perfect sand beach but it did nothing of the sort. Instead, she got this strange sense of absolute detachment. For the first time in her life she realized there would be a point when Nat wasn't going to be there. They were actually going to part.

"Jessie, why did you say that?" Liz asked.

"Because it's over. Isn't it, Hilton? If Nat thinks Hilton is still hanging on she'll be back."

"She's right," Hilton said. "And I'm okay with that."

Anne returned. "That didn't go in the direction I planned."

Hilton smiled, knowing the sentiment well. "What did he say?"

"He basically told me that my opinion has been noted. The dysfunctional nature of his family, however, was none of my concern. I guess he's got a point."

"Percy is a pretty cold fish," Liz said. "I had a political science seminar once and he came to speak. It was like he wasn't human. Sorry, Hilton."

"Like I care," Hilton responded.

The black limo started to creep down the road toward them. The tinted back window slid down. "Hilton?" Percy croaked from inside. "I gave Ms. Counterman's suggestions some review. Perhaps it is time we end this little feud of ours. Would you like to come to dinner at the house?"

Hilton stared at him. He was a lot older than she remembered him and a considerable amount frailer. She did the math. He would be sixty-six now. His gray hair was reduced to a few thin spots around the sides. He looked old and creepy. She replied, "I can't."

"Can't or won't?" His steely blue gaze met her own.

"I can't. Gran made me swear before she died that I would never see you again."

"Deathbed promises can be most bothersome and slightly impertinent, considering the person issuing them won't be around to see the results. Did she tell you why?"

"Yes."

"What did she say?"

"It's not very pleasant."

"Grant me the unpleasantry."

It was once again a battle of wills on the same beach that had changed all their lives forever. Only this time she wasn't a six-year-old girl standing next to the bloated corpse of her mother. She had power this time. "Gran said you were evil and you destroyed the lives of anyone who loved you."

"I see," Percy's bony white hand curled over the edge of the window.

"We wouldn't have anything to talk about anyway," she said diplomatically, suddenly feeling he needed the opportunity to save face.

He declined to take it. "There's always the weather. Next year, then." The tinted window went back up and the limo drove off.

"What the fuck does that mean?" Jessie snapped. "It's gray for the rest of the winter, and if you don't watch it you'll grow mushrooms on the top of your head from all the fucking rain."

"I almost felt sorry for him," Hilton said.

"You're like the million-dollar baby. Gran bought you from him. He chose money over his own kid. What kind of man does that?" Jessie said indignantly.

"I know. I overheard them the night Percy signed over custody. He needed money and she wanted to protect me. He'd never admit that." The picture was still fresh in her mind. The cracked door of the den and Percy yelling at Gran. She'd run to her room and later Percy came up and kissed her forehead. She pretended to be asleep.

"Hilton, are you all right?" Anne asked quietly.

"Yeah, I'm not like him, am I?"

"No, not ever. You have your mother's heart and your grandmother's soul," Liz said quietly.

"Maybe you do have some of his emotional detachment," Jessie said. "Ouch!" she said as Liz stepped on her foot. "And you don't trust a lot of people," she continued. Liz stepped on her foot again. "Damn it, do you not know my foot is there?" She glared at Liz.

"I'm trying to get you to shut your big fat mouth."

"No, Liz, she's right. I don't give myself over easily."

Anne took her hand. "Discretion is not a bad thing, Hilton. Especially since you are who you are."

"She's right," Liz said.

"Besides, we've got your back," Jessie said. She sat down on the beach and removed her shoe. She rubbed her foot.

"Is it all right?" Liz asked as she peered down at it.

"You're the one that did it."

"I know that! But I can still be concerned. Sometimes brutal honesty is not always the best policy. Besides, Hilton is expanding her horizons. We have Anne now," Liz said.

"And Veronica and Melissa," Jessie chimed in. She put her shoe back on, obviously convinced the damaged appendage was going to survive. "Now, let's eat."

"Yes, let's," Hilton said, suddenly feeling much better. She had a new life now. The two people who'd caused her the most trouble were no longer lurking around her, unconsciously giving her pokes and prods just to see her react. She was over Nat, and she'd told Percy the truth. It couldn't get much better than that.

They all sat down on the big quilt. Jessie prepared the feast with Anne's help. The sun made a brief appearance and the seascape burst with a plethora of color. Hilton gazed out on Puget Sound and thought life was kind of like that, sometimes gray and depressing and then suddenly, out of nowhere it became bright and full of color. She wished her mother would have stuck around for those moments.

Chapter Twelve

Two weeks had passed since that day on the beach and Anne never ceased to wonder how fast time flies when you're actually enjoying yourself. She'd been working on Web ideas with Hilton, and they'd gone shopping together for an addition to Hilton's wardrobe, who had discovered that there were winter clothes. Anne thought perhaps Veronica, who was still madly in love with Jessie, had gotten to her. She'd seen them perusing a *Vogue* and an *Elle* magazine together. Shannon had survived another round with the groomer and Liz and Melissa were getting along famously. Life, up to this point, had been pleasant. Almost too pleasant. Something was bound to fuck it up.

By Thanksgiving day, the only thing getting her through it was the knowledge that she would be seeing Hilton and the girls afterward for drinks and five-card stud. She'd been saving her change all week. It was a Hilton house tradition that Gran had started and the girls diligently upheld. It appeared Gran hadn't believed in gambling, but cards required skill so she allowed it and, judging from the stories, reveled in a good game of poker.

After she stoically helped her mother peel potatoes and cut up celery and onions for the stuffing, she'd been released from KP to go and visit with her father in his study. He was sitting at his desk, smoking a cigar and reading the *New York Times*. He was muttering to himself. He looked up when he saw her. Anne had his green eyes and thick, brown hair, although his short beard and mustache had turned white. He always reminded her of a jovial-looking Ernest Hemingway.

"The *Times* has become a cesspool for hack journalism. It used to be a good paper until it started this political agenda hogwash. Yellow journalism at its worst. History really is circular."

"Then why do you read it?" Anne sat down in one of the burgundy wing back chairs. His study looked like a page straight out of *Architectural Digest*. Her mother had the uncanny ability to make every decorating project picture perfect. A brass nameplate on the desk read Malcolm Counterman, PhD Dark oak bookcases lined the room and were a testimony to his intellectual prowess. Anne doubted her father even noticed the absolute correctness of his study, how his wife had thought of every detail of what the study of a Doctor of Political Science should look like. Her system of organizing their lives had worked out until her daughter lost her husband to another man. This turn of events didn't bode well in Brochure Land.

"I don't know. I just always have. It's like an old friend that's gone off the deep end but you can't cut yourself loose."

Anne laughed.

"So how's the book coming?" he asked.

"Shh, you're the only one who knows." She stole a look at the door. Her mother was a notorious eavesdropper.

"So how's it coming?" he whispered when she gave him the thumbs-up signal, indicating the coast was clear.

"I write a couple of pages a day and hopefully they'll accumulate into something like a novel."

"Ah, the doctrine of incrementalism. It's becoming a lost art in today's culture, which is a pity because small steps will eventually get you there. I think the Victorians were the ones who perfected it. They had the moral fortitude along with the luxury of time to know that Rome wasn't built in a day. This business of living in the fast lane will be our demise."

Anne smiled at him. He was the only one who ever understood her aspirations, first the radio career and now her desire to write thrillers. She'd always toyed with the idea but it was her father's gentle prodding that got her started. Before he'd retired five years ago he wrote papers for think tanks and op-ed columns, and although his imagination wasn't as fanciful as hers, at least they shared some literary leanings.

She asked, "Is it bad to achieve one's dream only to become disenchanted with the end product?"

"No, I think it's the normal landscape for overachievers." He looked at her over the top of his black reading glasses.

"I'm changing."

"Precisely."

Anne's mother retrieved them for dinner. As her father carved the turkey, Anne poured the wine, dreading the inquisition to come. She knew it was hiding somewhere between the mashed potatoes, the cranberries in orange sauce and the biscuits. She couldn't see it holding out until the pumpkin pie. Her mother hit her while she was passing the butter.

"Gerald called the other day."

"He did?" Anne responded innocently. She looked at the biscuit she had just finished buttering. A second earlier it looked appetizing, all fluffy and moist. It was no wonder she'd been thin most of her life. Her mother always chose the dinner hour to engage in verbal calisthenics.

"Gerald wanted to know if we would mind if you had your birthday dinner at his house rather than celebrating it here with us as we usually do, that perhaps we could take you out for lunch instead. I think it was very considerate of him. I have no problem with the change. He wants to invite you and your friend."

Anne, who had just bitten into her biscuit, swallowed wrong and nearly choked. "He told you about Hilton?" She could feel her heart begin to pound in her ears.

Her father handed her a glass of water. "Are you all right? Your face is all red."

"I'm fine."

"I think his inviting you to dinner is a really good thing," her mother said.

"You do?"

"I think it's very positive that he wants to see you and he says your new girlfriend had been beneficial for you. Oh, I'm so pleased." She clasped her hands together and beamed blissfully at her daughter.

Anne studied her mother's face. She wasn't getting the correct picture, which was often the case. Her mother was once again living in the illusion of her own desires. This was the first time it occurred to Anne that if she allowed herself to fall in love with Hilton that Victoria Anne Counterman was going to have a coronary.

"Yes, Hilton is very nice and we have a lot of fun together." Anne passed her father the cranberries. He hadn't indicated he wanted them but she didn't care. He politely took the dish.

"I just think it's a step in the right direction. Perhaps Gerald has done some soul-searching and you've become less myopic." A sweet smile played on her mother's lips.

"Excuse me?"

"Don't get your feathers all ruffled. I'm simply pointing out that you tend to be little too focused on what you want and what you're doing, with little regard to the needs of others."

"Which, of course, would have included my husband."

"I'm just saying—"

"Victoria, I think Anne has had enough motherly advice for one visit. It's a holiday, perhaps we can celebrate instead of denigrate."

"I think that's an outstanding idea, Dad."

"I'm not doing that!"

"You know, I've really got to go. Dinner was great as usual." Anne got up and pushed her chair back in.

"Where are you going?" Victoria asked.

"I've got some work to do to prep for the show tomorrow." She avoided her father's gaze. He would know this wasn't true but it didn't matter. She didn't want to fight with her mother.

Anne grabbed her coat from the bench in the hallway. She had started out the door when she discovered her car keys were nowhere to be found. Hilton kept threatening to get her one of those beeping key locators. She wished she had it right now. She retraced her steps and eventually found them on the kitchen counter. The kitchen was adjacent to the dining room and was separated by a swinging wooden door. Anne could hear her parents talking.

"Victoria, this is hardly her fault," her father said.

"She must have done something. Gerald is the sweetest man."

"He's still a nice fellow and Anne wasn't the one who turned him out. She can't really compete, you know."

"I don't know what you mean."

Anne could easily envision the look on her mother's face. It would be one of consternation coupled with blatant stubbornness, a refusal to see the world as it was instead of how she preferred it to be.

"Anne doesn't have a penis."

"Malcolm, don't use that word. It's disgusting."

Anne wanted to run in there and dance around the table like an errant five-year-old screaming, "I don't have a penis." Instead, she softly chuckled, put her car keys in the pocket of the leather coat and slipped out of the house. Her father always stood his ground for her and now she knew that whatever happened between her and Hilton, her father would handle it. Her mother would be the bigot she always was, but her father would stand by his daughter.

Anne got in the car and turned on the radio, hoping there would be something on the news that would distract her. This was a futile cause, as nothing really exciting was reported on a holiday. Everyone was supposed to be relaxing and enjoying their family time. She tried to quiet her fury as she drove across town. She didn't want to arrive at Hilton's in a heap of tangled emotions. The twenty-minute drive helped. She felt relatively calm as she pulled up in front of Hilton's house.

She looked at her watch. It was only six-thirty and the rainy day had now turned pitch dark. The house looked warm and inviting. She was certain the house would be appropriately decorated with Veronica in charge. She imagined white linens, tapered candles in silver holders and little nameplates at each setting. She smiled.

Hilton opened the door. She looked pleasantly surprised. "You're early."

"I walked out on dinner," Anne said, ramming her hands in her coat pockets. She could do that now that her thumbnail had fallen off. The house was filled with the smell of food. Her stomach tugged at her. Now she was hungry.

"Didn't go so well, huh?"

"Not exactly."

"We're still eating, so come eat, have a glass of wine and forget about your mother."

"How'd you know it was my mother?"

"Because I've read your father's op-ed pieces online. The dude rocks."

Her father was a guest columnist for a popular online news site. Anne knew he was never fully satisfied unless he was writing and making social commentary. It was just nice that now he could do it at his leisure without the pressure of a deadline. "I overheard him telling my mom that it's not my fault I don't have a penis and that's what Gerald wants."

They both laughed. They went to the dining room. Liz got up and gave Anne a warm hug.

"Let me get you a plate," Liz said.

Anne walked by and popped Veronica on the head as a sort of greeting. Veronica actually smiled and said, "And how are the illustrious Victoria and Malcolm Counterman?"

"Lovely as ever," Anne said, taking a seat. Veronica had met her parents several times at the radio station. The long dining room table was decorated just as she imagined it. Veronica must have dug around in the china cabinet for all the good dinnerware. It was a picture-perfect Thanksgiving table. She must have made some apparel decisions as well. Hilton was dressed in a long, black dress coat with a white ruffled blouse and the others looked well-turned-out in sweaters and blouses.

"Parents can really suck sometimes, but they're responsible for the women we love," Jessie said. She took Veronica's hand and nibbled at her fingers.

"Jessie, that was so sweet," Liz said. She set Anne's plate down.

Hilton handed her the turkey platter. Anne took two slices of turkey and then a good-sized dollop of mashed potatoes. Jessie passed her the cranberries.

"She's right, though," Melissa said. She squeezed Liz's thigh.

"Boy, mark this day on the calendar," Jessie said. She smiled big.

"Exactly. It will be noted that on this day, Jessie said something sweet and appropriate," Hilton said. She poured Anne a glass of Pinot Noir. Anne nodded her appreciation. She felt better already.

"So how is everyone else's family on holidays?" Anne inquired. She took a sip of wine. She needed some moral support. Here was a group of women and none of them were spending the day with their parents. She wondered why.

"Oh, I don't think you want to know," Jessie said. "It's not a pretty picture."

"Jessie maintains family relations through a series of religious pamphlets that her parents send from Portland. They even highlight the pertinent parts in case she misses the point," Liz explained.

"The burn-in-hell parts," Jessie added. "I think it's designed to diminish my fragile self-image. It hasn't worked yet." She puffed up her chest and put her arms behind her head. "Sometimes I get a wild hair up my ass and send them a note with something like 'God made all creatures so he must have made me.'"

"Then we get boxes of literature," Liz said.

Anne laughed. At least her mother wouldn't use the God card. She was more concerned with what her peers would think than what the Almighty would do to her errant daughter. "How about you?" she asked Liz.

"We adhere to the stoic, Midwestern decorum utilized by the Armed Forces—don't ask, don't tell. They don't ask about boyfriends and I don't tell about girlfriends. We keep it to serious discussions of the weather."

Hilton took her hand under the table and squeezed it as if to convey that everything would be all right. They really needed to have a talk. Was she truly capable of changing her entire outlook on the world and the world's outlook on her? This was a little more serious than just falling in love. This was turning your whole life upside down with the hope that it would eventually work itself out.

"If it's any consolation, Melissa has really cool parents. They even belong to PFLAG," Liz said.

"What's that?" Anne asked.

"Parents for Lesbians and Gays," Melissa explained. "And they really like Liz." She beamed at Liz.

Hilton topped off Anne's wineglass and handed her a linen napkin and a fork. Anne realized she hadn't touched her food yet. "Is that a hint?"

"Yes, you need to eat something."

Veronica piped up. "I'm a fourth-generation lesbian."

"What the hell does that mean?" Jessie said. She handed Hilton the cornbread stuffing. Hilton plopped some on Anne's plate.

Anne couldn't decide if Hilton was trying to distract her from the subject at hand or if she was truly concerned about her caloric intake.

"It means my great-grandmother was a suffragette and an ardent lesbian. My grandmother was raised as a lesbian and so was my mother, who in turn educated me."

"But what about the biological angle?" Anne asked. She took a bite of stuffing.

"There were always helpful men, lesbian-identified men who

were willing to supply the necessary ingredient." Veronica shrugged.

"Oh, my, your family sounds like modern-day Amazons," Anne said.

"Precisely, and we're extremely proud of our family tree and hope to continue the tradition," Veronica said. She stared intently at Jessie.

"Would I make a good father?" Jessie asked.

Anne stifled a laugh. She noticed Hilton and Liz both had their mouths open. Veronica appeared not to notice. Jessie gave them a dirty look.

"With proper training and guidance you'll make an outstanding parent," Veronica said, patting her hand reassuringly.

Anne cut her turkey and took a bite. It was delicious. They all grew quiet as they ate dinner. Anne had two glasses of wine, cooed over Veronica's homemade biscuits and generally enjoyed her dinner. Her earlier dinner became a distant memory. Hilton kept shoving food at her until she adamantly refused.

"All right then," Hilton said. "Let's finish this up and get the poker game going."

"I've been saving my change all week," Anne said.

"Do you know how?" Hilton asked. She got up and pulled a box of cigars out of one of the hutches that lined the ornate dining room.

"Never played it before in my life," Anne said, making sure to keep a straight face.

Hilton smiled. "Watch this one, everybody. We may have a master bluffer in our midst."

They cleared the dining room table and then retired to the library, where one corner of the room had been converted for poker, right down to the green felt-covered octagonal table.

"Did Jessie decorate this room too?" Anne asked. The library was carpeted in a dark burgundy Berber and the rest of the room was filled with heavy oak end tables and brown leather chairs along with two couches. It looked like something out of a high-class men's club. Amber cut-glass crystal ashtrays sat on all the end tables, and the heavy club-footed coffee table that separated the two couches contained leather-bound books on fox hunting, English gardens, and Roman architecture.

"She did," Hilton said. She lit a cigar and handed it to Anne.

"Wow!" Anne said. She sucked slowly on the cigar.

"I saw the whole thing in this home and garden magazine on English country style and I copied it, right down to the books. I call it the Man Room."

Melissa plopped down in one of the chairs. "This rocks."

"Thanks."

"I think she should take interior design classes," Veronica said.

"Let the games begin," Hilton said. She pulled out a fresh pack of cards and they all took their places at the table to try their luck.

Anne couldn't help thinking this was the most fun she'd had on a holiday. Perhaps being an abomination and a social pariah wasn't going to be that bad at all. She liked Hilton's friends and there never seemed to be a dull moment. Victoria Anne Counterman was just going to have to get over it. Anne sucked her cigar and studied her cards.

Chapter Thirteen

One week after Thanksgiving Anne stood staring in the full-length mirror in the bedroom. She had just finished showering. Today was her fortieth birthday and she was surveying the damage. She kind of wished this year her birthday had fallen on a Friday or Saturday night so she could party and then start the weekend. She decided she didn't look so bad for someone her age. Her breasts were still perky, her arms had muscle tone and her stomach wasn't puffy like a lot of her married-with-kids friends. She ran her hand down her stomach and toward her groin, wondering what it would be like to have a woman touch her, or more specifically, to have Hilton touch her. Was it greedy or stupid to think that she could have two great loves in her lifetime? She had loved Gerald so deeply that at one point she couldn't have imagined her life without him in it, but now her feelings for Hilton ran deep as well. Did this mean that love was transferable, that all the joy and pain of what you thought was your one great love could occur again? It was this part that frightened her.

She got dressed, having decided on her charcoal gray wool pantsuit with a black silk blouse. It was one of her favorite winter outfits. It was a typical cold rainy day, so she wouldn't be too warmly dressed. She tried not to think about bad gag gifts and black balloons, to be followed by a lunch date with her parents. She hoped Victoria would abstain from discussing Gerald. She didn't want another fight like on Thanksgiving. Birthdays were serious. They were meant to be points of reference and reflection on what a person was doing with her life and where her life could go in the future. She knew this birthday was one of bifurcation, the quintessential fork in the road. This next year of her life would determine more things about her life than any others and she didn't want edible underwear and tacky comments on aging to shroud its importance. If she was changing sides of the sexual preference fence she needed to face it with seriousness she had yet to know.

When she got to the office Ed met her at the door with a card. "Just a little something to get you through the day," he said. He winked at her and left her to her day. In the studio she found a dozen red roses and the place filled with helium balloons. Not one of them was black.

Hilton, Dave, Veronica—even Liz and Jessie, who had obviously taken the morning off from school—all sang "Happy Birthday." Jessie inhaled some helium and sang the final verse in a Chipmunk-style crescendo.

Lillian walked in and looked around. "What's this?" she asked suspiciously.

"It's Anne's birthday," Hilton said.

"Earth Day, what a stupid holiday. Nothing but a bunch of kooks trying to take our money. The whole group of them are nothing but a bunch of leftover Commie bastards. I dated one once. Horrible man—didn't bathe, didn't shave," Lillian muttered. On the way to the control room she snagged a cup of sparkling cider and eyed the angel food cake that Veronica had made.

"What is she talking about?" Hilton asked Anne.

"Environmentalists. She hates them. It has something to do

with the Alaskan Pipeline, mating caribou and an Eskimo," Anne replied in Chipmunk talk. Jessie had given her a quick lesson on how to inhale just enough to get through a couple sentences. Anne wondered if she'd spend her lunch hour with the helium tank. That would really irritate her mother.

Hilton laughed. "Happy birthday." She gave her a hug.

"I suppose you're the one responsible for this little soiree?" Anne whispered in her ear.

"I had a lot of help."

Dave did the honors. "So, we all chipped in and got you a little something." He handed her a small box wrapped in silver paper with a red bow.

Flattered, Anne opened it. People didn't usually do things like this for her. She was always the one who arranged parties and sent flowers. It felt kind of odd and yet special to be on the receiving end. Inside the box was an iPod. "Hey, this is neat." She stuck an ear bud in.

"You can scroll down like this," Hilton said, showing her how. "Dave downloaded all your favorite bumper music, you know, the whole song."

Jessie handed her another box. "This is from the girls at the house."

Anne tried not blush at the pleasant surprise. She opened it to find an electronic key locator. "You didn't."

"I've never known anyone that loses their car keys so much. Here, hand them over and we'll see if this thing works," Jessie said, holding out her hand.

Anne frisked her pockets. She couldn't find them.

"Are you serious?" Hilton said. She started to laugh.

Veronica picked them up off the reception desk counter. "Here they are."

Anne laughed. "Okay, I guess I really do need one."

"Let's have cake," Jessie suggested.

"Is that all she ever thinks about?" Anne asked. She took the knife from Veronica and cut the cake. There were no candles and she thought that was tasteful.

"No, there's one other thing," Hilton replied.

Veronica blushed at the implication.

Anne handed Jessie the first piece. "Veronica, this looks stunning."

"Thank you. It's one of my specialties."

"Wait until you taste it. She let me sample the filling. I didn't know cherries could taste like that," Jessie said.

"Jessie, you better watch your backside if you keep hanging out with Veronica," Hilton said.

"Not with the gym and our extracurricular activities," Jessie said.

"We're taking a cycle spinning class together. You wouldn't believe the amount of calories you can burn pedaling your brains out," Veronica said.

"Yeah, and in our class you get to watch reruns of *the L Word*. On the big-screen television no less," Jessie added.

Liz rolled her eyes, "As we were saying—her stomach and her nether regions."

"Nether regions?" Jessie asked.

Liz pointed to her crotch.

"Oh, that."

They all laughed.

Anne centered that day's radio show around the best and worst birthdays. Why not? she reasoned. There were some poignant stories from the callers—the romantic balloon ride to getting dumped on your birthday. After the show Anne's parents came by to take her to a late lunch. Later on she and Hilton were going to Gerald's for dinner.

"Hilton, I want you to meet my parents," Anne said, drawing her near.

Hilton shook hands with both of them.

Victoria eyed her intently. "Hilton, you look familiar. What's your last name?"

"It's probably from the billboard all over town that advertises the cast of the radio program," Anne said.

"No, I don't think so," Victoria said, her eyes narrowing.

"It's Withers isn't it?" her father said innocently.

Anne gave him a look that he obviously didn't get. She wanted to keep Hilton's identity quiet for a little while until some things had ironed themselves out.

"Hilton Withers. Aren't you Senator Percy Withers estranged, lesbian, heiress daughter?"

"Yeah, that'd be me."

"Funny, Gerald didn't mention that," Victoria said.

Anne smiled at her. *That's because he's too polite. I don't introduce you as my control-freak, psychotic, tactless mother even though that's what you are.* "It probably slipped his mind," she said sweetly.

"Why doesn't Hilton come to lunch with us?" Malcolm said.

"I don't think that's a good idea. I'm already taxing her for dinner tonight with the boys," Anne said.

Hilton looked distinctly uncomfortable.

"You know, let me go to the restroom and then we'll go," Anne said.

Anne left and Malcolm said to Hilton, "I really like what you've done with the Web site. I think it definitely enhances the program. This new trend, it's very spot on."

"Thank you, Mr. Counterman."

"Call me Malcolm." He winked at her. "I have a feeling we'll be seeing a lot of you."

"All right, Malcolm."

"I think the Web cam is changing the face of radio. It's like the new formatting style of FM; they're using the train-wreck method of running all kinds of music together."

"You know a lot about radio."

"I love it as a medium, and of course I listen because of Anne's show. But it has to evolve in order to keep vibrant."

"Like in the early eighties when everyone thought MTV would kill radio. Instead some songs made it big because the video was so good," Hilton said.

"Precisely," Malcolm said, beaming at her.

Victoria was still staring at her like she was an alien. Her cell phone rang. She pulled it off her belt. "Excuse me," she said as she turned away.

It was Anne. "I don't want you to think I didn't want you to come to lunch. It's just my mother."

"You worry too much. Everything will be fine."

"Okay, I'll pick you up at six."

"Great. You know, I'm looking forward to this."

"Really?"

"Yes. Are you always this weird on your birthday?"

"Yes, be kind to me."

Hilton laughed. She couldn't wait for tonight. She had an extra-special present for Anne and she wanted to meet Gerald. She couldn't help but wonder what kind of person Anne had loved.

Anne came by promptly at six. She had changed from her charcoal gray suit to linen pants and a yellow cashmere V-necked sweater. Hilton had decided after much contemplation on black leather pants and a white silk shirt that Liz had kindly ironed for her.

"You look nice," Anne said.

"I wouldn't want Gerald to think you were hanging out with a slob," Hilton said, grabbing her coat and checking her breast pocket for Anne's present. She picked up the two bottles of Cabernet Sauvignon that she'd chosen earlier and placed in the foyer.

"Is Shannon going to be okay with this?" Anne asked as they made their way to the car.

"Yeah, she's hanging out with the girls. They're going to watch this movie called *Good Boy*. It's about a boy and a dog that's from outer space. Jessie is into appropriate movies when she baby-sits. I think Shannon is just really interested in the huge hambone I got her."

"Great, thanks for doing this. I'm not sure I'd go if it wasn't for you." Anne started the Chevy Avalanche. She was about to drive off when Hilton stopped her.

"Wait, I want to give you something."

"Another present?" Anne said, raising her eyebrow.

"This is a me-to-you kind of present." Hilton avoided her gaze as she handed her the box.

"What's this?"

"Open it and see." This time Hilton looked at her. She wanted to kiss her and whisper, "I love you—okay, I admit it, I love you," but she knew she'd do neither. She took a deep breath and smiled. "I hope you like it."

"Hilton, it's beautiful." Anne pulled the ladies Rolex watch out of the plush jewelry box. "And very expensive."

"I'm an heiress, remember." Hilton had spent a solid week searching jewelry stores for the ultimate one. She'd finally decided on a thin gold band with an oyster-shell face and a small diamond inset at twelve o'clock.

Anne slipped it on her wrist and then held it out to admire it. "You know, sometimes I actually forget. Wow, this is awesome."

"It looks good on you."

"How'd you know I've always wanted one?"

"All lesbians have the ability to read secret desires. It comes with the territory." She was teasing but wished it was true. She wanted to peek in Anne's brain and search the place that held her desires, shuffle around a bit and find one with her name on it, like rummaging through the sale rack and locating the one treasure it contained.

Anne furrowed her brow. "You're joking, right?"

"Why? Are you hiding something?"

"Other than a secret desire for a Rolex?"

"Yes."

"You'll have to wait and see."

She wrapped her arms around Hilton and held her. "Thank you."

A hundred erotic images raced through Hilton's brain but caution ultimately won out, screaming in panic, "Be careful, be careful, don't mess this up." It was like there were yellow caution signs everywhere telling her to let Anne lead the way.

When they got to Gerald and Philip's immaculate and tasteful house, Hilton whispered, "He really is a fag." The yellow bungalow had a large front porch complete with a swing. The yard was well cared for and terra-cotta pots lined the stairs up to the porch. They contained topiary plants.

"I know," Anne said. She handed Gerald her leather coat and white scarf.

Philip came to greet them. His blond hair was spiky on top and his high cheekbones and thin nose all contributed to his good looks. He was wearing a blue-and-white twill apron over khaki slacks and a dark blue dress shirt with the sleeves rolled up. "Hilton, it's been so long. You look great. Gerald was surprised I knew you. I told him, 'How many dykes do you know named Hilton who makes money from pickles.'"

"Uh, yeah, that'd be me. Philip, I haven't seen you in ages." She hadn't equated Anne's description of him with the grad student she'd met during one of the Queer Nation protests. She'd liked him. He seemed sweet and intelligent.

He gave her a big hug. Anne looked quizzically at Hilton.

"No, all gay people do not all know each other," Hilton said.

"She's teaching me things," Anne said.

Gerald and Philip stood holding hands and looking at the two of them with what seemed like fraternal warmth. Hilton studied their gaze. Did they look like they wanted them to be together or was she imagining it? This was like the ten other questions she asked herself every day about her relationship with Anne, starting with was this the beginning of a love affair or simply her desire to make it so?

"Hilton and I worked together, or rather volunteered, for some Queer Nation stuff," Philip explained to Anne.

"Yeah, we got really good with a staple gun," Hilton replied.

"Speaking of staple guns, how's your thumb?" Gerald asked.

"It's fine," Anne said, sticking her hand in her pocket.

"Let's go have a drink in the living room," Gerald suggested.

"I'll drop the wine off in the kitchen with Philip, who needs to check on things, I'm sure," Hilton said. She really needed to talk to him.

"Perfect," Gerald said. "Anne and I will pour drinks and await your arrival."

When Hilton and Philip were safely in the kitchen, Hilton said, "Tell me I'm not nuts." She set the wine on the granite countertop. The kitchen had a black-and-white checkered floor and all the appliances were stainless steel. There was a huge rack of copper pans hanging over the kitchen island.

"Clinically or metaphorically?" Philip chided. He opened the oven door and peeked in. She could see the rack of lamb. He had obviously braised it, reassembled the rack and wrapped the bottom half of it in tin foil. Her grandmother had done it much the same way. It was always delicious. Hilton hoped this was a good sign for a successful evening. She wanted Anne's birthday to be as perfect as possible.

"Philip, I need your help."

He turned around. "I know. She's been to talk to Gerald."

"About what?" She could feel her heart begin to race. This was like the quintessential moment of truth. Were her hopes to be scattered? She took a deep breath.

"About you, silly." Apparently satisfied with the progress of dinner he turned his full attention to her.

"Really?"

"Really. Look, I was in your situation once and it's freaky, but you two already act like you've got the U-Haul hitched to the car."

"What if I'm imagining this and she's just one of those touchy-feely kind of straight women."

"Anne Counterman?" he said, raising an eyebrow.

"All right, that's not exactly how I'd characterize her," she conceded. "So how do I go from point A to point B?"

"Oh, this is perfect. I'll have Gerald tell the story of us over dinner—that'll get the ball rolling," he said mischievously.

"Oh, I get it. This is a recruitment dinner."

"We don't recruit the unwilling." Philip looked at the bottles of wine. "Very nice. Still have the wine cellar, I see."

Hilton smiled. "Stocked to hilt."

He touched her shoulder. "Don't worry, for as bad as you've got it, she's got it worse."

"Okay." She could feel herself relaxing.

"Come on, let's go see what they're up to."

The first thing Hilton noticed at the long mahogany dinner table was that everything matched—the napkins and the table-cloth, the glasses, the silverware. If she and Anne did do the U-Haul thing they'd have matching accessories. She actually liked what Jessie was doing with the house. It had class. It had style. She was ready for that now. Nat hated shit like that because it reminded her of her upbringing, and Gran always thought it was pretentious and overrated. Couldn't pleasantries be a part of their lives without being showy?

"That's a nice watch," Gerald commented as he carved up the lamb.

Hilton studied him for a moment. He was an attractive man, well-dressed in that elegant, understated way. He was everything Hilton would imagine Anne had wanted in a man.

"It was a present from Hilton," Anne said, looking at her instead of him.

That was a good sign, Hilton thought. She put some of the mint pesto on her pepper-crusted lamb and told Philip that he was an outstanding cook. The lamb was cooked to perfection. She'd never had lamb with mint pesto but it added to the flavor. The new potatoes and peas with pearl onions all accented the meal.

He passed her fresh rolls and beamed at her. "Gerald, it appears that Hilton is interested in our story as well."

"Is that all right with you?" Gerald asked Anne.

"Hello, I've been trying to get this story out of you for the last year," Anne said.

Hilton took her hand under the table. She wasn't sure if Anne was expressing false bravado or if she wanted to know, as Hilton did, how one crossed the line.

"So it goes like this . . ." Philip prodded.

"This is difficult. I don't really know exactly how it starts. We're friends. We do guy stuff together . . . a lot. Philip didn't tell me he was gay for a long time, and when he did it didn't matter. Guys can be kind of weird about that stuff. Then there comes this day, this time, and it all seems right, it all makes sense and then you jump," Gerald said. He had been looking at Philip but now he looked at Anne.

"And then you come home, pack your clothes and tell your wife you're gay," Anne said.

"I knew storytime wasn't a good idea," Gerald said. He took a sip of wine.

"At least it's out in the open now," Philip said cheerfully.

Hilton was mortified that Philip's plan had seemingly gone awry. It wasn't what she had intended.

"It's fine. I'm fine. I'm glad you found the love of your life and your true self," Anne said diplomatically.

Gerald looked relieved.

Hilton watched as Anne also seemed to relax. She had two glasses of wine and seconds on the new potatoes. She took this to be a good sign.

After dinner Philip dimmed the lights and went to the kitchen to get the dessert. He came out with key lime pie and four candles. "I thought cake might be too heavy after lamb and Gerald said key lime was your favorite." Philip's cheeks were highly colored and Hilton could tell he wanted to make this work.

"You can do the math," Gerald said gently.

Anne smiled. "And I still look fabulous."

"Incredible," Hilton said.

Anne took a deep breath and blew out all the candles. Philip cut the pie expertly and handed out the slices.

Hilton took a bite. "It's delicious."

"Thank you. Oh, we have a present for the birthday girl." He pulled a beautifully wrapped box from the chair next to him and handed it to Anne.

Gerald smiled at her benevolently. "I hope you like it."

"There's a demonstration after you open it," Philip said.

Anne opened the box. Inside was an ornately cut crystal bowl. She pulled it out carefully and examined it. "It's beautiful."

"Okay, now wait." Philip took the bowl and disappeared into the kitchen. Gerald dimmed the lights until the room was almost dark. Philip brought the bowl back in. It was filled with water and had small scented tea candles floating in it. The crystal glowed with light. He set it down before Anne. "It's for romantic dinners." He looked pointedly at the two of them.

"How nice, isn't it, Hilton?" Anne said.

"Lovely," Hilton replied. She tried to imagine romantic dinners with Anne. Was she capable of being romantic? She hadn't learned much from Nat, whose idea of romance was to fling you on the floor and fuck you silly. Perhaps she'd quiz Anne on what she envisioned as romance.

After dinner, they had brandy in the living room. Philip and Hilton told them Queer Nation stories. Both Gerald and Anne wiped their eyes a couple of times from laughing.

"I'm thinking I didn't miss much," Gerald said. He sipped his brandy and smiled at Anne.

"No, my first experience with a staple gun wasn't that successful," Anne said. She looked down at her thumb.

Gerald glanced over. "Will the nail grow back eventually?"

"What are you implying, that it looks like the head of a penis?" Anne asked.

Philip leaned over to look at. He was sitting on the couch next to her. "Yes, as a matter of fact, it does."

"Well, don't worry, boys, I won't be competition for you. It's going to grow back," Anne said.

Hilton smirked.

Later in the car, Anne looked over at Hilton. "Do you think Philip is a bit of a control freak?"

Hilton, who had been sucking on an after-dinner mint that Philip had insisted they have from a vintage silver tray he kept in the entryway, was taken aback. She started to laugh, almost choked, then sent the dinner mint projectile-style into the windshield. It bounced back and landed neatly in her lap. "Gee, what makes you think that?"

It was Anne's turn to laugh. "I thought you were going to put your eye out with that thing."

Hilton opened the car window and flicked the mint outside. She hadn't wanted it in the first place, but Philip was so insistent she'd felt obligated. "You know, I simply asked Philip how he got together with Gerald. I didn't expect him to tell the story in front of you. I would never do that to you."

Anne stopped at the light. She took Hilton's hand. "I knew that. It was territorial of him."

"Good. I felt bad."

"You don't have to. I'm not like that, right?" Anne turned onto the expressway.

"Not like what?"

"A control freak," Anne said.

"Uh, no. You're kind of the opposite. You have a control freak for a producer, you have a slacker for a broadcast engineer and a deaf call screener. That is like the most uncontrolled work environment I've ever seen and I like it. It pretty much sums up your personality. Some people like control freaks. They feel safer with someone who can take care of things. Look at Jessie."

Anne pulled into Hilton's driveway. "What do you want in a relationship?"

"Vaginal sobriety."

Anne laughed. "Now, that's an original term."

Hilton looked at her. "What do you want in a relationship?"

Anne was silent for a moment. "I want to be that special some-one that your lover wants to come home to, wants to wake up next to, wants to share your dreams with, that's what I want."

"That's beautiful. Do you want to come in? It's only ten." Hilton hoped she appeared casual and not pleading, but it seemed that tonight was the night for the big jump.

"Please, I need to unwind. Can I see the wine cellar?"

"Of course," Hilton said.

When they got inside Liz and Jessie were lounging on the couch watching a DVD of last season's *the L Word*. This was Jessie's new obsession, but it did beat out reruns of old shows on cable. One more episode of June and Ward Cleaver and she was going to scream.

"I'm telling you, they had to bring her down like that. It's like the classic Greek hero who falls in those bullshit stories," Jessie said.

"You did learn something in college," Liz said.

"What are you talking about?" Hilton asked.

Anne sat down on the ottoman and stared at the television. Two of the characters were seriously going at it.

"How Bette ended up screwing around on Tina," Liz said.

"See, Bette was always the one playing high and mighty and it's all about the rules and monogamy. Then bam, the hot carpenter chick comes along and all Bette's morals go flying out the window," Jessie said.

"If she'd been smart she never would have hired her because Bette knew that she was attracted. If you want to keep it together, don't tempt yourself," Liz said.

"Because lust always wins out?" Anne inquired. She had man-aged to pry herself from the television.

"Let's go see the wine cellar," Hilton suggested, noticing that Anne's curiosity seemed a little more than academic.

"Can't we just finish this part?" Anne said. She tilted her head to one side as she studied the position of the two women on the screen making love.

Hilton gave Liz a look. Liz grabbed the remote and flipped it to the blue screen. "I think that's enough for one night."

"Where's Shannon?" Hilton asked, suddenly aware that her dog was nowhere in sight.

"Oh, you've got to see this," Liz said, getting up. "She's in my bedroom."

Liz and Hilton were about to leave the room when Jessie flicked the show back on and Anne went to sit by her. Hilton frowned at Jessie.

"It's tasteful," Jessie said.

"No, it's borderline porn," Hilton replied. She didn't want Anne's first look at lesbian sex to be on cable. She'd kind of envisioned showing her the ropes in a sensual setting at just the right moment.

They went down the hall to Liz's room. Shannon was sleeping on an old sheet with her paw tucked protectively around her bone.

"Isn't that sweet?" Liz said.

"She's a good dog."

"How was dinner?" Liz asked quietly.

"It was fine. Gerald is a nice man."

"That's it?" Liz said, raising her eyebrow.

"All right, he's really good-looking, smart, and well-mannered." Hilton sat on the bed and stroked Shannon's head.

"He's not your competition, you know."

"You're right, of course. It's just kind of hard meeting someone's ex-husband."

"Did Anne like her present?" Liz leaned in the doorframe. Hilton could tell she was being studied.

"Very much." Hilton smiled at the thought of it.

"You love her, don't you?"

"Is it that obvious?" Hilton asked nervously.

"Only when you're together," Liz teased.

"I want this to work out," Hilton said, looking intently at Liz as if she might have some clues written on her face.

"It will. Shall we leave her?" Liz asked, pointing to Shannon.

"If it's all right with you."

"That dog is the best electric blanket on the planet."

160

Hilton agreed and they rejoined the others.

"Wow, I had no idea," Anne said. Jessie was apparently pointing out some of the finer points of the show.

Hilton could only imagine. "Let's do the tour," she suggested.

"Sure," Anne said. She popped up instantly.

They went downstairs to the wine cellar. Anne stood in the middle of the room lined with cabinets full of bottles. Recessed lighting gave the room a warm glow.

"This is amazing."

"It was one of Gran's joys. She taught me everything and left behind a wicked reorder list so it'll never be lacking." Hilton picked out a Concha y Tora Cabernet Sauvignon and grabbed two wineglasses from a rack that hung over the bar. "I've been saving this for a special occasion. It's from Chile and it rocks."

"For us?" Anne said.

"But of course. Let's go to the cottage and really celebrate your birthday," Hilton said. She could have sworn Anne was almost being flirty.

"You mean without stress?"

"And dinner mints on silver trays," Hilton said.

"Oh, we forgot about my lovely lunch."

"How did that go?"

"My mother spent an entire two hours quizzing me about you."

"Do I have that much of a biography?"

"She seems to think you do."

They slipped out the kitchen door to the cottage, where Hilton put on a Nora Jones CD and poured the wine. Anne sat on the bed and propped the overstuffed pillow behind her. She looked quite comfortable. Hilton handed her a glass of wine.

Anne took a sip and then another sip. "Oh my, this is absolutely marvelous."

"I'm glad you like it." Hilton sat next to her. She wanted to tell Anne that she loved her, that she wanted a life together, to really be a couple and make a future, but she didn't know how. The only other woman she'd loved was Nat and the only time she uttered those words was flat on her back having the daylights fucked out of her. She couldn't envision that with Anne and didn't want to.

"Hilton," Anne said, breaking her train of thought, "I really like spending time with you."

"I'm glad." Hilton blanched, berating herself for finding the lamest response on the face of the earth. *You'll have to do better than that, you idiot.*

Anne stroked her cheek. "And this is the best birthday, dinner mints and all, that I've ever had, thanks to you."

"Anne . . ." Hilton started to say.

"Just hold me for a minute."

Hilton put her face against Anne's smooth, lightly-scented neck and tried not to think about what it might be like to kiss her neck, her throat, her breast.

Anne took Hilton's face in her hands. Hilton could see that her pupils were dilated, and she remembered a class in Medieval literature. Ladies, she learned, took belladonna to dilate their pupils so it would appear they were always interested in their suitors. She was certain this was the moment. Anne would kiss her now.

"I've got to go," Anne said. She got up abruptly.

Hilton was still in her about-to-be-kissed mode and Anne was out the door before she had a chance to utter one syllable in protest. Instead, she sat there feeling like her heart had just been expertly extracted from her chest. Her throat got tight and she had that same sinking black feeling that occurred when her mother died, when Gran got sick and the day Nat moved out. It was like she was almost happy and then something awful happened. She lay back on the bed and let the tears come. She wished Shannon was there. She would nestle her face in her soft white fur and listen to her even breathing and go to sleep and forget this all happened. She knew she was expected to reinsert her mutilated organ and go on with life forgetting that what was red and glowing with love was now black with the death of her dream. She didn't think this was going to be possible. She curled up and prayed for sleep.

Chapter Fourteen

The next morning Anne was sitting in the booth waiting for the show to start. She didn't feel social so she pretended to be working. She was really waiting for Hilton to show up so she could talk to her about last night. She kept replaying her gross error. She should have kissed Hilton. They should have been holding each other and waking up in a tangle of covers. Instead, she woke up alone and regretted her lost chance.

At ten minutes to the top of the hour Hilton showed. Apparently she'd called Dave and gotten the Web site up and running via her home network. Anne had always been in awe of Hilton's computer skills, but today they were not working in her favor. She couldn't decide if Hilton had had a messed-up morning or if she was making a point to avoid her. She had a feeling it was the latter. She called the control room and asked Hilton to come in. Anne could tell she was angry and hurt.

"I am so sorry about last night. I didn't mean to do that. I botched it big-time and I know that," Anne blathered as Hilton stood there cold as a stone. This was going to take more than an apology and more than six-and-a-half minutes.

"It's fine," Hilton said. She ran her finger along the corner of Anne's desk, clearly unwilling to look at her.

"That wasn't how it was supposed to happen."

"It's fine. Perfectly understandable," Hilton said matter-of-factly. She looked at the clock.

"I know. Can we talk later?"

"I'd better go check on my computer."

Anne knew she should probably wrap Hilton up in her arms, kiss her and profusely exclaim her love and desire. Then take the rest of the day off. Instead, Dave tapped on the window and pointed at the clock.

"I know, I know," Anne said.

"I gotta go," Hilton said.

The show was like living in purgatory. Hilton was sullen and nothing Anne did could make her smile. It was the longest show in Anne's life. Finally it was over and Anne came racing out of the studio. She looked at Dave. "Where is she?"

"She bailed. She put the Web site on some kind of auto-pilot. Is something going on?" He ran his fingers through his hair and looked nervous.

"Everything's fine," Anne said. She took off for the parking garage but Hilton's pea-green Bug was gone. Anne dialed her cell phone and got no answer. She'd go to the house and prostrate herself on the front lawn and beg for forgiveness.

Liz was just getting ready to leave for class when Anne pulled up at twelve-thirty. "Hey, what's up?" She slung her bookbag in the passenger seat of her beat-up black Toyota truck.

"I'm trying to find Hilton. She's gone missing after last night's faux pas."

"What happened? I mean, you don't have to talk about it if you don't want to."

"No, I need to. I need some advice. I'm really out of my league here."

"We all are in the beginning," Liz said. Her face echoed her concern. "It'll all work itself out."

"I don't know. Hilton is pretty hurt and angry with me." She shoved her hands in the pockets of her suede jacket.

"Let's go sit on the stoop and you tell me what happened."

"Do you have time?"

"I'll make time. Come on," Liz took Anne's hand and led her to the porch. It was a rare blue-sky day and it was brisk. They sat on the steps.

"Well, you know that moment when you think everybody is going to kiss and the romance starts . . ." She picked up a fallen leaf and twirled the stem between her fingers.

"Yes."

"We were talking and then it was that time and I freaked."

"What did you do when you freaked?"

"I was about to kiss her and then I got up and left, rather abruptly." Anne looked up from the leaf and met Liz's gaze.

"Like she had her eyes closed and puckering?"

"Kind of like that." She ran her hand across her forehead and squeezed her temples. "I truly fucked up. This is horrible."

"No, it's not that bad. It's not good, but it can be repaired." Liz put her arm around Anne's shoulders.

"How do you know that?"

"Because Hilton is madly in love with you and when she gets through licking her wounds, she'll be back around."

"But I snubbed her."

"Yes, but once she figures out it was nerves and not denial she'll come running. Trust me."

"How's she going to figure that out if she won't talk to me?"

"I'll make sure she does."

"Really?" Anne didn't feel so confident.

"Hilton doesn't give her heart lightly. How she feels about you isn't going to fade in an afternoon."

Anne nodded. "I'm going to go home, stay calm and wait." She said this more to herself than to Liz.

"Very good idea."

Anne didn't burst into tears until she got into the house. After an hour she made herself a drink, a nice stiff gin and tonic, lay on the couch and waited. Waited for the phone to ring, a knock on the door, a message from above. She finally fell asleep convinced her love affair was over before it had ever really begun.

Hilton sat in the parking lot of the local McDonald's feeding Shannon french fries and sipping black coffee. She was cold to her very core. They'd spent the afternoon at the beach. They were the only ones there. A cold Thursday afternoon in December was not prime beach-going time. Shannon chased gulls and Hilton watched the cold, gray waves come rolling into the equally gray shoreline. The only change in color was the frothy, white line of the surf as it met the sand. Shannon had devoured two cheeseburgers and was hungrily munching the french fries. It was nearly six-thirty and she decided it was safe to go home. She didn't want to face Anne and she figured by now she'd long given up on her coming over and making amends. She'd had an entire afternoon to ruminate and it hadn't lessened how she felt.

The house was dark when she pulled in. She was hoping that Liz and Jessie were both out with their respective new partners. She and Shannon slipped quietly around back to the cottage, which was dark as well. "I think we're in the clear," Hilton told Shannon. She opened the door and stepped on something kind of hard, but squishy, and the something screamed. She flipped on the light. Jessie was lying on the floor.

"I think you crushed an internal organ or something," Jessie said. She was holding her stomach.

Hilton switched on the Tiffany lamp by the bed and then turned off the overhead light. She hated that light. It was too bright and made the whole cottage seem rather garish. "What are you doing on the floor?"

Jessie grabbed her wrist and slapped on a pair of handcuffs and then clicked them into a brass ring attached to the side of the bed. It happened so fast she didn't have time to react. She just stood there stunned. She went to pull away and tripped on the heavy drill Jessie had left on the floor, stubbing her toe.

"Watch out for the drill," Jessie warned.

"It's a little late for that," she said, wincing. "What the hell are you doing? And look what you did to my bed." She pointed to the brass ring bolted into the side of her waterbed.

"It was great improvisation. Look, it's an old sash holder I found in the shed." She pulled Hilton's arm. "See, it works great."

"But why am I being held hostage?" Hilton sat down on the bed as that seemed the only way she could be somewhat comfortable. Standing there with her arm attached to her bed was hurting her lower back.

"In a minute," Jessie said. She dialed her cell phone. "Mission accomplished."

Liz came out immediately.

"What? Were you guarding the house?" Hilton asked.

"Yes," Liz confessed. She noted the handcuffs. "Jessie, what have you done?"

"You told me to make sure I kept her here. So that's what I did."

"Jessie, I think your measures might be just a little over the top." Liz sat on the bed next to Hilton. Shannon apparently decided it was all too much for her and she went to her bed in the corner of the room, letting out a heavy sigh.

"What exactly are you two up to?" Hilton asked. She took off her shoe and sock and examined her big toe, the one she stubbed on the drill.

"It's called an intervention. We're trying to save you from yourself," Jessie said.

"What's wrong with your toe?" Liz asked, peering down at it.

"I tripped over the drill Jessie left lying around."

Liz frowned at Jessie. "It was an accident," Jessie said defensively.

"Hilton, Anne is madly in love with you. She freaked and, frankly, considering she's switching sides, you could have been a little more supportive instead of acting like the demure, passive woman you imagine yourself to be," Liz said.

"That was brutal," Jessie said to Liz.

"No, it's honest."

"You really should have jumped her bones. What's with this playing Cinderella crap and waiting to be kissed. Where are the huevos rancheros, baby?"

Hilton got up to leave and was snapped back into place.

"See, I told you we'd need restraints," Jessie said.

"Hilton, calm down," Liz said.

Hilton sat back down. "She really told you that she loves me?"

"Yes, she came by looking for you and she was extremely upset. We had a talk. It's not about denial. She was scared."

"I see. It's all so weird. I thought we were on the same page and then bam—she bails. What was I supposed to think?"

"Love is always whacked like that, but running off and not letting her explain, that's kind of harsh," Jessie said. She went to the beer fridge. "You got any beer in here? I'm feeling a little jangled. I've gone from sound asleep to having my organs stepped on to the fucking Spanish Inquisition."

"Can I have one?" Hilton asked. She was sort of feeling the same way.

"Come and get it," Jessie said holding up a bottle of Rolling Rock.

"Jessie, that's mean," Liz reprimanded.

"I'm thinking being handcuffed to my bed has got to be a violation of my civil rights," Hilton said.

"Jessie, unlock her."

Jessie handed Hilton her beer. "Not until we get the correct response out of her."

"Which is?" Hilton asked. She tried to get the bottle cap off the beer but it was proving difficult with one hand cuffed.

"Here, let me," Liz offered. She opened the bottle and handed it back to Hilton.

"The correct response is you're going to tell Anne how you feel and apologize for being such a crass asshole and then you're going to live happily ever after," Jessie said.

"But now it's all weird. Can't I just kiss her instead?"

"That'll probably do it," Liz said.

"The only thing that concerns me is what if after a couple of months she decides this gay thing isn't really her scene?" Hilton had sat on the beach all day studying all sides of this wily conundrum that loving Anne had proposed.

"Hilton, how many hasbians do you know?" Liz asked dryly.

Jessie lay back on the bed and rubbed her stomach. "I'm hungry."

"None." Hilton thought back to all the conversions she'd ever known and not one of those women had ever gone back to men. It was like once they made that leap they lived happily ever after in Homoslavia even if they didn't stay with the first woman who kissed them. Surely that counted for something.

"Can we get a pizza?" Jessie asked.

"Is that all you ever think about?" Liz reprimanded.

"Yes. Well, I mean I can have sympathetic moments, but Hilton really did botch this one up."

"Jessie!" Liz reprimanded.

"No, she's right. It is my fault," Hilton said woefully.

"Hilton, don't give up on love. It's a nice thing. I almost did that and it would have been a tragic error," Liz said.

"I won't. I promise. Let's get a pizza and drink some beer. I'll go see her in the morning." Hilton put her beer down and pulled the cell phone from her pocket. "I could dial a lot faster if I had my good hand."

Jessie unlocked the handcuffs. Hilton ordered two large pepperoni pizzas.

"Happy now?"

"Happy, very happy." Jessie reached over and kissed her on the cheek. "We really need to appreciate this time because our lives are really going to start changing with the introduction of new people and new commitments that we've not known before."

Hilton and Liz broke out in mad fits of laughter.

"What?" Jessie said.

"It's like you're possessed," Hilton said. She pinned Jessie to the bed and sat on her chest. "Jessie, are you in there. Come back, Jessie. I think the aliens have abducted her."

"What are you talking about?" Jessie asked. She tried to wrestle free but Hilton was stronger.

"You almost sounded like a grownup. It was pretty scary," Liz said.

Chapter Fifteen

The morning light filtered through the half-drawn curtain and it danced across Hilton's face. She was plucked from some weird-ass dream that was reminiscent of a Greek tragedy where the soldier sails home from battle and he is supposed to change the color of the sail from black to white so his beloved will know that he arrived home safe. He forgets and she sees the black sail and jumps off the cliff into the sea below. Hilton glanced at the clock. It was eight-thirty. Jessie and Liz lay curled up next to her. Last night had been quite the slumber party. They'd stayed up until four in the morning drinking beer and eating pepperoni pizza.

Hilton crept out of bed and went to pee. She washed her face and quickly brushed her teeth. If she hurried she could get to studio and still have a chance to talk to Anne before the show started. Then they could go have a good talk.

"Holy shit!" Jessie bolted upright. She rubbed her eyes. "What the hell time is it?"

"It's late." Hilton grabbed her coat, kissed Shannon on the forehead and said, "Jessie, can you watch her?" She gestured to the dog.

"I'm so there for you."

Hilton bolted. Luckily, traffic was smooth. It seemed that on Wednesdays and Fridays half the city called in sick so the street-to-car ratio was dramatically reduced. Once she reached the office she took the stairs because the elevators were jammed up with last-minute workers trying to make it on time. When she got into the office Veronica and Dave both looked agitated. Dave was nervously running his fingers through his hair and Veronica was stacking and restacking papers. Hilton flew past them. Anne wasn't in the booth.

"Where is she?" Hilton said, turning to face both of them.

"She called in. We're going to play a best-of tape," Dave said. "And I've got a good one. I've been compiling all the funny ones over the last four months."

"You need to fix this and fast," Veronica said.

"How?"

"I've been pondering this all morning. You've botched all your other avenues so you need to go to her—with flowers—and prostrate yourself." Veronica peered at her and then pointed to a spot on her jacket. "What's that?"

Hilton looked at the spot and then peeled off a piece of pepperoni. "It's pepperoni from last night's pizza."

Veronica sniffed her. "You smell like a beer parlor. Oh, this will never do. Both of you come with me."

Dave looked at Hilton and shrugged. They followed Veronica to the executive washroom.

Veronica extracted a key from her blazer pocket. "Dave, wait here. Hilton, come with me." Once inside the marble-tiled washroom, Veronica said, "Okay, take them off."

"Excuse me?"

"Your clothes. I'm sending them downstairs to be martinized. You can't go pledge your love looking like a transient coming straight off a drinking binge." Veronica opened a locker and pulled out a toiletry kit. She unwrapped a fresh toothbrush and handed it to Hilton, who had removed most of her clothing. Veronica got her a towel and pointed to the showers. She handed Hilton's clothes to Dave with the instructions that they were to be cleaned immediately, in eight minutes or less, and he was to run to the florist around the corner and get a dozen yellow roses. "Don't get a vase. Anne will have a vase and it's always a woman's secret pleasure to look for it while she blushes about the flowers."

Hilton tried not to snicker as she overheard this conversation. She slipped into the shower and wondered as the warm water ran down her body if Veronica's plan was really going to work.

Her clothes arrived seconds after she got out of the shower. Veronica insisted she should fix Hilton's hair. "I think we should tie it back in a ribbon so you or preferably Anne can pull it out and your lovely locks can come cascading down. It's so romantic."

Hilton felt like a Barbie Doll with Veronica writing the script. When she finally got in her car, she immediately pulled the ribbon out and vigorously wiped off the lip gloss. It took her thirty minutes to get from downtown to Anne's eastside house. There was some huge accident and she'd been forced to hit the side streets instead of using the expressway. She still remembered the night she'd gone to her house, the night Nat and Emily had gotten in the catfight in the front yard. She was thinking that was when the whole thing started. That was the day she'd started to fall in love.

The one-story bungalow was quainter than she remembered. The house was the color of beach sand and had a light green shingled roof and trim that matched. The porch had dark green wicker chairs and a matching coffee table. It looked like it could be in *Sunset* magazine.

Anne's Chevy Avalanche was parked in the drive. It was too large to fit in the tiny garage of the house. Hilton parked her car, took three deep breaths, grabbed the flowers and prepared to meet her fate. She knocked on the door. It seemed an eternity before Anne answered. Hilton could tell she'd been crying. It was at that moment the last chink in her defenses crumbled to the ground. She handed Anne the roses. "I'm so sorry."

"They're beautiful. Come in." She led Hilton back to the kitchen. She was dressed in blue jeans and a gray fleece pullover with a white T-shirt underneath. It was the first time Hilton had ever seen her without dress clothes on. She looked smaller and suddenly fragile. Hilton wanted to scoop her up and kiss away all the hurt she had caused. She was still thinking about this while Anne located a vase. Hilton watched as Anne's shoulders started to shake and quiver. She was crying. Hilton came to her.

"What's wrong?"

"They're yellow."

"I thought you liked yellow."

"They stand for friendship," Anne said. She wiped her tears with her sleeve.

"Oh." She was going to kill Veronica. For all her fucking planning she screwed up the most important part. "Veronica made me get them, after she made me take a shower and have my entire outfit martinized—whatever the hell that is, and then she put a ribbon in my hair and lip gloss on. It was all perfectly disgusting." When Anne started to laugh, Hilton held her. "I thought you didn't want me."

"No, I was scared." Anne pulled away and looked at her. "I'm so in love with you that it frightens me."

Hilton kissed her, softly at first and then passionately as Anne responded in kind. She ran her hands down Anne's sides and across her hips, then pulled her in closer. Anne wrapped one of her legs around Hilton's and moaned softly.

"Do you want to go somewhere more comfortable?" Hilton asked. The last time she was at the house she'd seen most of it but not Anne's bedroom. She was certain it would be as beautifully decorated as the rest of the house.

"Please." Anne took her hand and led her to the bedroom.

They stood by the bed. It was a four-poster bed in cherry wood with huge pillows and a yellow down comforter. Hilton was now certain yellow was Anne's favorite color. Hilton unbuttoned her shirt. She wasn't wearing a bra. Then she took Anne's hand and placed it on her breast, watching her face the entire time. Anne traced the outline of Hilton's nipple. Her hand was soft and warm. Hilton guided Anne's hand down her stomach and in between her legs, expertly slipping under her waistband and boxers. Anne made a little noise, like the kind Shannon did when she was extremely happy about something, and didn't appear to need any further coaching.

She pulled Hilton close and slipped her fingers inside. Hilton shuddered for a moment at her touch. She took off Anne's pullover and then her T-shirt. She ran one hand under Anne's black bra and undid the back of it with the other. As she unbuttoned Anne's jeans and slid them down her slim hips, Anne removed her hand from between Hilton's legs and did the same. Anne took her panties off and pulled at Hilton's boxers until they both stood naked.

"You don't know how long I've been waiting for this moment," Hilton said.

"You have," Anne teased.

Hilton smiled. Anne was back to her normal, sassy self. Hilton gently pushed her back onto the bed. "I have." She eased down on top of Anne and kissed her ardently. Their bodies fit together almost perfectly. Hilton kissed her shoulders and then bit one. "That's for being a smart ass."

Anne laughed. "You like me that way."

"I do," Hilton said, looking up at her as she cupped Anne's breast. Goose bumps rose on Anne's skin. Hilton raised her eyebrows. "Ticklish, are we?"

"Maybe just a little," Anne conceded.

Hilton kissed her stomach and then opened her legs, slowly running her tongue between the wetness that waited for her. Anne rose up to meet her and moaned softly. When Hilton thought she was almost there, she put her fingers inside her and moved up to kiss Anne's face. "Is this all right?"

"Oh, my God."

Hilton took that as a yes. She felt Anne reach for her and they moved together. Hilton felt Anne come in an explosive orgasm. Hilton held her, feeling her body quiver. Making love had never felt like this before. Hilton smiled. They both opened their eyes at the same time.

"Wow," Anne said.

"Double wow. I love you. You know that, right?" She gazed at her.

Anne held her tight. "Yes."

"No regrets?" Hilton asked as she nestled between Anne's breasts and listened to her heartbeat.

"Actually, I do have one."

Mortified, Hilton looked up at her. "What?"

"That we didn't do this sooner."

"Oh, you're in for it now." She went to tickle Anne but Anne was faster. She flipped Hilton on her back, held her down for a moment and then stared at Hilton. Hilton knew that look. She'd seen it before. It was the realization that the object of your desire can be yours, wants to be yours, and that you can be the aggressor.

Anne kissed her passionately. "I was supposed to do this the other night." She reached for Hilton's nipple.

"Yep. It would have saved us a lot of time."

Hilton felt Anne part her legs and kiss between, sticking her tongue inside with little teasing thrusts. Hilton moaned. After a while, Anne turned her on her stomach and took her from behind. Hilton rocked against her and then reached back for Anne. Soon they were both making noises that Hilton wagered neither of them had made before. It was the moment before she came that Hilton knew she had found her one true love.

It was dark when Hilton awoke with Anne's warm body beside her under the down comforter. She silently crept from the bed. Looking out the bedroom window she could see that the day's rain had left everything shiny. A street light illuminated the side yard of

Anne's house. She drew the cover over Anne's bare shoulders. Gazing at her for a moment before leaving the room, she felt the most intense series of emotions—love and longing wrapped up with complete devotion, and it was then that she had another epiphany, like the one last summer when she realized she was growing up. Suddenly, she wanted to scoop Anne up in her arms and scream, "I love you!" She knew this was lunacy and would probably scare the living daylights out of her lover. She wished there was some way she could prove her love, to show her the molecules of her heart filled with love. Hilton took a deep breath and told herself to get a grip.

They had made love all afternoon, something neither of them confessed to having ever done before. They talked, they laughed, they kissed, and they explored every inch of the other's body and then finally fell asleep in each other's arms as the soft rain danced on the rooftop.

And now, hours later, Hilton, wearing only a blouse, crept into the kitchen and was poking around in the fridge looking for food. The pizza last night was the only nourishment she'd had. She was starving. The fridge was rather bare, containing mostly condiments and every kind of pickle imaginable, including a jar of Wither's Pickles. Hilton chuckled softly to herself. Anne never mentioned that she liked pickles. She guessed there were a lot of things they'd discover about each other as time went on. The mischievous nature of the universe never ceased to amaze her—a pickle heiress and her pickle-loving girlfriend.

Soft footsteps came padding down the hall. Hilton smiled warmly at Anne. "You don't have any food except condiments and pickles, lots of pickles."

"I meant to go shopping but I was kind of depressed."

"Most people eat when they're depressed. Why were you depressed?"

"Because I thought I'd lost the love of my life."

"No, the love of your life was being a complete idiot and should have been more clear about how she was feeling."

Anne laughed. "Okay, if you say so, but I really think it was my fault for being a coward."

Hilton closed the fridge, having come up empty-handed. They'd have to order out. "How about Chinese food?"

"Sounds fabulous." Anne was sitting on a barstool at the kitchen island. She was staring at her. "I can't believe you're my girlfriend."

Hilton put her hand out across the counter. Anne took it and guided her around to her. She pulled her in close. Anne caressed Hilton's thighs. Hilton could have melted right there. She was going to have to learn to control herself or they'd be spending the rest of their lives in bed. Smiling, she thought that might not be such a bad thing, but she did want more. "I'd like to be your wife . . . someday."

"Is this about vaginal sobriety?"

"Yes." Hilton stared at her.

Anne kissed her lightly and held her. "Then consider this an I do."

Hilton kissed her forehead. "Food, we need food, then we'll start the honeymoon."

Anne pouted. She pulled a tattered menu from the kitchen drawer. Hilton quickly perused the offerings and called in the order. "We have forty minutes."

"We can do a lot in forty minutes," Anne said, leading her to the couch in the living room.

Chapter Sixteen

On Sunday afternoon, Liz called and persuaded them to come for dinner. She had teased Hilton that they had to come out of the bedroom sooner or later. She was making vegetable ProvenVal with couscous and onion tarts. Veronica and Melissa were also coming for dinner. Hilton was nervous. It was easy to spend the weekend in each other's arms but going out in public was to begin their life together with all of the unknown challenges.

Anne must have sensed this because she took Hilton's hand and said, "I could spend the rest of my life here but we can't, and we will deal with things—including my mother."

Hilton took a deep breath.

"It will be fine," Anne said. She got up from the bed. "Come have a shower with me."

"Is that like an interim activity?"

"Precisely."

❦

Later that evening Hilton and Anne were in the living room picking out music. Once the CD player was loaded, Hilton wrapped her arms around Anne's waist and they danced slow to the music.

"This was the most incredible weekend of my life," Anne said.

"Me too." Hilton kissed her passionately.

There was a tussle in the hallway and someone said, "Let go of me."

"Nat, don't go in there," Jessie said.

Hilton pulled away from Anne and glanced up. She felt her stomach drop. She knew she had to tell Nat but she didn't want it to be today.

Nat was standing in the doorway staring at her. "So you're banging the boss. Is that what this is all about?"

"Nat, I tried to warn you," Jessie said, tossing her hands in the air for emphasis.

Hilton took Anne's hand and faced her ex-girlfriend. Several phrases came to mind, most of them far from polite, so Hilton opted for the stripped-bare truth. "Yes, Anne and I are in love."

"What about us?" Nat demanded. She placed her hands on her hips.

Hilton looked at her for a moment. She had hip-hugger jeans on, a tight green shirt and a motorcycle jacket. She was the same girl Hilton had always loved but it was different now. Hilton felt detached. It was as if Nat was a rowboat that had once been moored to her dock and she'd just untied it, watching the rope float on top of the water as the boat drifted listlessly away.

"Nat, there hasn't been a relationship since you went to live with Sherry."

"You guys fucking remodel the house. It's like I was never here," Nat ranted.

"Why are you here?"

"It's our fucking anniversary," Nat said. She threw a burgundy jewelry box at Hilton, who just barely managed to catch it before it nailed her in the face.

"What the hell? Nat, let's go talk on the porch, okay?" Hilton glanced at Anne.

"Go talk. You two don't need an audience," Anne said. "I'll go help Liz chop vegetables."

"Forget the vegetables, let's have a stiff drink," Jessie suggested.

Nat and Hilton sat on the porch. Hilton was still holding the small box. "Nat, what are you really doing here?" It was true, it was their anniversary but Hilton could count on one hand the number of times they had observed it. She knew Nat had something else on her mind. Hilton took her hand.

"I'm not sure I want it to be over," Nat said.

"Are you done with Sherry?"

"Not exactly, but Sherry wants this commitment thing. She's not like you."

Hilton watched as Nat looked down at their intertwined hands. "Good for her."

"I don't know if I can do it."

"You want me back so you can resume your old ways. Nat, how much fresh meat do you need? How many positions can you do it in? It's all finite. Maybe it's time to explore commitment. It might do you some good." Hilton looked at the box. "What's in it?"

"It's a ring."

"I'm not the one you should be giving it to."

"So that's it then? We're done? You're in love with the boss lady."

Hilton nodded.

"What happened to Emily? I thought you two were hanging out." Nat was standing now, holding the jewelry box in her clenched fist.

Hilton knew Nat wasn't going to take this lying down. She needed to make her realize that they had separate lives now. "We only slept together that one weekend."

"So the whole time I've been away you've been falling in love with her," Nat said, pointing to the living room. Tears were welling up in Nat's eyes.

"Something like that."

"That's just fucking great. You've all been lying to me," Nat shouted hoarsely.

"Nat, come here."

"No, don't touch me. Liars!" She raced down the driveway toward her little white car and screeched away.

Hilton went back inside. "That didn't go well."

Liz and Anne looked at her sympathetically. Veronica and Melissa came in the kitchen door. They were laughing and joking about something. They stopped when they saw everyone's somber faces.

"What's wrong?" Veronica asked. She took Jessie's hand.

"It's Hilton's anniversary," Jessie said.

"But you two just got together," Melissa said.

"No, Nat and Hilton's anniversary. Nat just came by and found out about them. It wasn't pretty," Jessie explained.

"Oh, I'm sorry," Veronica said. "Do you have a vase?" She pulled a bouquet of red and white dahlias from the paper bag she was holding. "I thought we needed to some color in this gray season."

Liz pulled a vase from the cabinet above the fridge. "How about this?"

"Perfect," Veronica said. She set to arranging the flowers.

Anne gave Hilton a hug. "Are you all right?"

"It's not me I'm worried about. I've been long over it."

Veronica said, "Well, the way I see it, Nat is a slut who gets what she deserves."

"Veronica!" Anne reprimanded.

"No, she's right. Nat has played around on me for years. It's her turn to get dumped," Hilton said. She jammed her hands in her pockets and wondered how anger and pity could possibly be intertwined.

After dinner that night in the cottage, Anne lay wrapped in Hilton's arms. "I never want to spend a single night without you," she said.

"That's part of the I do," Hilton replied, running her fingers through Anne's hair.

"I do, I do, and I do."

Hilton looked down at her. "You know, we're going to have to be careful." Ever since Nat made an appearance, she couldn't stop concocting horrible scenarios that would force the two of them apart—Anne's parents, her job, second thoughts about being gay. The possibilities were endless.

"Because of the show?"

"That, as well as your parents." Hilton watched her face carefully.

"I know, and we'll make it work." She looked determined.

Hilton felt a sense of temporary relief. When Anne set her mind to something she didn't flag when things got tough. "I think Malcolm already gets it." She liked him. It was Victoria that concerned her.

"Really?"

"Really."

"Well, your background buys a lot of stock in Victoria's world."

"I hope so. It's not going to be easy. You know that, right?"

"All I know is that I've never felt this way about anyone, including Gerald. You are first and foremost in my life now and the rest is details that will have to be worked out."

"I could think of a detail or two that needs to be attended to," Hilton said. She took Anne's hand and put it between her legs.

The next morning Hilton lay in bed watching Anne sleep. It was still early but she couldn't sleep. She tried to lie still so as not to wake Anne. Shannon was sleeping on her side of the bed. Hilton listened to her even breathing, hoping it would relax and comfort her as it had so many nights before when she was scared or sad. She normally looked forward to going to work, seeing Anne work her magic with the callers and her particular take on the day, but today was different. She could feel it. Nat wasn't going down without a fight.

Hilton had spent years trying to figure out how Nat operated. She had compiled much data but had yet to discover any sort of pattern of behavior. Nat was as unpredictable today as she was ten years ago. This was an alarming fact, and until Nat acted Hilton was living on a precipice waiting for the shove. If Nat did anything to hurt Anne, she would retaliate. What she feared was that Nat would destroy her relationship with Anne, and knowing she would hate Nat from that moment forward made the whole thing worse. Everyone would end up alone.

Anne stirred, fluttered her eyelids and woke up. "Good morning. Are you all right?" She was staring at Hilton.

"I'm fine, really."

"You don't look fine. What's wrong?" Anne straightened out a tangled lock of hair and rubbed sleep out of her eyes. Hilton could tell she was attempting to function as quickly as possible.

"It's not an imminent crisis," Hilton reassured her. "Today is our first day in the real world and I'm a little nervous."

"Oh, well, don't be. I won't kiss you in public. Dave knows, Lillian is oblivious, and Ed won't find out until I tell him and we'll decide how to deal with it then. Ed is most likely going to say it's our business and don't advertise. No one knew my husband left me for another man. Some things people don't need to know." Anne rolled back into Hilton's arms. "Now, how much time do we have?"

"About ten minutes before the alarm goes off."

"Oh, too bad. Let's go shower at my house, grab a coffee on the way."

"All right," Hilton said. She wished Anne's confidence would rub off on her. Shannon jumped on the bed and looked at her expectantly. "Need to go out?" Shannon barked. The day had begun.

On the way to Anne's house, they listened to the national news and Anne played around with several ideas. The day was windy with high clouds. It didn't look like rain but the sun was nowhere in sight. Hilton was attempting to comb the knots out of her hair before she showered.

"I know, let's do a show on what it's like to live in a gray cloud for four months. It could be a discussion of coping mechanisms," Anne said enthusiastically. "What do you think?"

"Sounds great," Hilton said, looking out the window. "Or maybe we could call in sick and run off to Mexico where's it's sunny all the time."

Anne laughed. "I can't wait for our first vacation together." She turned the radio to a music station and tapped her fingers on the steering wheel in time to the music.

Hilton reached back and patted Shannon's head. Shannon sighed contentedly. Why was she so tense when her lover and her dog were happy as clams? You shouldn't worry so much, she told herself. Nat was probably getting banged right now and not giving her a thought. Perhaps she was suffering from some sort of post-traumatic love syndrome. Everything seemed too good to be true so disaster must be lurking somewhere. Anne knew how to handle things and Hilton knew she would. She leaned back in the seat and gazed at Anne. At the stoplight Anne reached over and kissed her. Hilton stroked her inner thigh and kissed her ear.

"Let's see how fast we can get into the shower," Anne said, her breathing growing ragged.

"You're on." She started to unbutton her shirt. Anne's eyes got big. "Don't worry, my jacket will cover it up."

Ten minutes later, as the water cascaded over both their bodies, Hilton ran her hand through Anne's hair as she knelt. Hilton felt Anne's tongue run across her clitoris and she moaned softly. Anne slipped her fingers inside her, then stood up, pulling Hilton near. "I wanted to do this earlier," Anne whispered.

Hilton caressed Anne's breast and slid her hand lower. Anne spread her legs wider and Hilton gently stroked her. Anne moved closer and then cupped her hand over Hilton's, pushing her farther inside.

"Oh, yes, like that, just like that," Anne said.

"We're going to be late for work," Hilton said as she gyrated her hips against Anne's hand. She felt her orgasm rip through her.

"No, we're not," Anne said, pulling Hilton in tight her body quivering. "Yes."

They held each other for a moment. The cold water started trickling through.

"We better hurry. We're almost out of hot water," Anne said.

They got ready for work and Hilton felt better. Just holding Anne made her feel better. They would get more coffee at McDonald's and an egg sandwich for Shannon, go to work, get some lunch and spend the rest of the day in front of Anne's fireplace having a good glass of wine and doing nice things to each other. It was going to be all right. Hilton smiled at Anne as they got on the expressway and started downtown.

"I love you," Anne said.

Hilton took her hand and kissed her cheek.

The radio show started as usual. Anne began her monologue on how to survive the winter in Seattle. People called in with their take on the subject. Hilton's favorite caller was the New Age one.

"It's necessary to embrace the grayness, dance in the rain, sip herbal tea and do yoga so your joints don't stiffen up from all the dampness."

"That sounds great," Anne said, throwing a pencil in the ceiling. "Maybe a little slow for me, but it takes all kinds."

Another guy called and said, "I just visualize the mushrooms growing on my head and I want to shoot my fridge because I'm going nuts."

"I'm with you," Anne said, twirling another pencil that was two seconds from hitting the ceiling.

Hilton could tell she was getting bored. They were five minutes from the bottom-of-the-hour news and weather. She grew relaxed as life appeared to be normal. She was probably just being paranoid.

Anne took another call. "Hello, caller, go ahead," she coached.

"I just wanted to talk about what I used to like to do in the winter."

"All right."

"Well, I had this lover and we used to cuddle up on the couch and have a glass of wine," the caller said.

Hilton recognized the voice. She looked at Anne, who hadn't made the connection. She was frantically trying to decide what to do.

"But I can't do that anymore because you stole my girlfriend and I'm thinking that's what you've been doing," Nat said.

"Well, Natalie, nice of you to call."

Hilton sprang from her seat. "Lillian, drop the call, drop the call," Hilton screamed.

Lillian couldn't hear her because of her headphones.

Dave swung around in his chair. "Hilton, what's wrong?"

"How does it feel to steal someone else's girlfriend?" Nat taunted.

"Drop the call!" Hilton screamed.

Lillian looked at her, plucked off her headphones and screamed back, "Don't tell me to chop-chop, young lady, I'm screening calls as fast as I damn well please." She slapped her headphones back on.

Hilton banged her head on the table. What the hell did Anne think she was doing? This was going to wreck her career instantaneously. Everything she feared was coming to fruition.

"Well, if you'd been a better partner that wouldn't have happened, but you were out screwing every Tina, Denise and Harriet in town," Anne retorted.

"That's your POV on the issue," Nat said. "She was still my girlfriend and you had no right."

"Nat, it's time you moved on. I love Hilton and we're in it for the long haul." Anne dropped the call.

Hilton was still banging her head when Dave put on the bottom-of-the-hour news and weather. Anne came into the control room followed by Veronica.

The first words out of Veronica's mouth were, "That fucking little bitch. Why didn't you drop the call? You should have dropped the call. And Lillian, what the hell were you doing? You know you officially outed yourself. Ed is going to kill us." She was standing with her hands on her hips in her usual tailored skirt and jacket.

"I was listening," Lillian said, stomping off to have a cigarette.

"That's just fucking great!" Veronica screamed. "You can't hear half the time but this time you were listening."

"Well, sometimes things happen for a reason," Anne said. She smiled broadly at Veronica.

"You know this is the end of your career," Veronica replied.

"Yes, I'm aware of that."

"Dude, I don't think this was a good move," Dave said, running his fingers through his hair.

"Actually, I'm kind of relieved. I have two years left on my contract and I'm sure I'll find something to do," Anne said, looking at Hilton. "You've got a black smudge on your forehead." She wet her forefinger and tried to rub it off.

"I'm so sorry. I had no idea she would do this."

"You know, I'm pretty much done with this part of my life. I was bored to death six months ago and then you came and maybe that's why I had to ride it out. But it's over now and why not go out with a bang." Anne clapped her hands and smiled. "Dave, let's get this show on the road."

Ed, the program director, stood in the doorway blocking her exit. He looked serious. "A heads-up would've been nice. I'm going to have a lot of explaining to do."

"Let me do one more segment," Anne pleaded.

"It's not going to be pleasant," he advised. "We could avoid the issue all together. Put Dave on the calls and not let anyone through with a homophobic or homosexual comment or we could do a best-of show and call it good."

"No, Ed, I have to live in this town and should at least get a chance to explain myself. Otherwise it'll always look like I'm a big closet case."

"They're going to hang me for this upstairs," Ed said. He stuck his hands in his trouser pockets and furrowed his brow. "Okay, here's how it's going to go, no screaming matches, and watch for profanity. I mean quick with the switch. I certainly hope you have a balls-to-the-wall monologue because you're going to need it."

"Oh, believe me, I do. Thanks, Ed."

He left. The control room was quiet. Shannon must have noticed because she came in and nuzzled Hilton's hand. "It's all right, girl," she said, petting her.

Veronica was suddenly beaming. "I've got a great idea. You could be a gay talk-show host on XM Satellite Radio. You'd be brilliant."

"No, thanks. I'm going to write thrillers."

"You write?" Hilton said. "All those yellow legal pads and the pencils . . ."

"You wrote a book?" Veronica said.

"I'm writing a book," Anne corrected.

"Dude, I want an autographed copy," Dave said.

"I know an agent. Well, I dated an agent once," Veronica said.

Lillian came clomping in. "So you're a lesbian now?"

"Yes, Lillian."

"I was a lesbian once," she sat down and looked reflective.

"Once?" Anne said.

"It was the summer of nineteen fifty-five . . ."

Dave, apparently not able to stomach the image of Lillian in the throes of girl-passion, cut the story. "I hate to interrupt but we better get this thing rolling."

Anne nodded. She touched Hilton's shoulder. "It's going to be fine, I promise."

"I'm not letting the bigots on the air," Lillian screamed from across the room as she sat down and clamped her headphones on.

"Thank you, Lillian," Anne said. "All right, boys and girls, let's rock and roll." She went into the booth and the bumper music started.

◈

189

After station identification Anne started her monologue. "As you all probably have deduced from that last segment, some things in my life have changed. I'm not certain as of yet how this will affect the remainder of my career but I will keep you posted. So in honor of that I'd like to welcome you to Homoslavia, my new homeland. It's a place where Fiesta Ware and the Pottery Barn rule all fashion, a place where parents hold their arms up in the air and wail, 'What have I done to deserve this? Where did I go wrong?' It's a land filled with Donna Summer tunes, pink drinks and rainbow flags adorning the porches of neat bungalows where couples still have sex in tastefully decorated bedrooms with designer sheets. Homoslavia, home of the free, home of the brave. And now it's your turn for all the bigotry and ugliness of the latent fears in your heart that you can muster. People, bring it on."

The first call was from her father. "Hi, Dad. This wasn't exactly how I planned on telling you."

He laughed. "Well, you always were for making a big splash and scaring all the little fish. I just wanted you to know I'm all right with it."

"How's Victoria taking it?"

"At the moment she's packing. I imagine she'll be hiding out in a spa in Palm Springs until this whole thing blows over." He chuckled.

"You got to love a woman with a brave heart."

"She'll get over it. Welcome to the family, Hilton."

Hilton smiled weakly. She still had the black smudge from the newspaper on her forehead.

The rest of the show was comprised of the burning-in-hell crowd, gay callers wishing her well and offering advice, a lawyer who threatened to sue the station on her behalf and supportive straight people who knew gay people or had gay relatives. Anne still threw pencils at the ceiling and when she was bored scribbled notes down about new scenes for her book. She was suddenly feeling very inspired. No pain, no gain—it didn't just apply to the gym. She was starting a new life now and she was kind of excited.

After the show, Anne said, "See, that wasn't so bad."

"You are a very brave woman," Hilton said. Anne noticed she'd washed the black smudge off.

"They can only hurt you if you let them." She hooked her arm through Hilton's and then said, "Let's go have a few cocktails. Everyone is invited. I want to toast my new life. I feel like a fucking butterfly who just dumped the white condo."

"I can finish my lesbo story," Lillian said, putting on a giant purple hat with a black feather. Dave ducked just in time to avoid having his eye poked out by the razor sharp end of the feather.

"Oh, great, I can hardly wait," Hilton said.

"No, please," Dave said, putting her hands together in prayer.

"Here. When she starts the story just put the ear buds in," Hilton said. She handed him her iPod.

"Sweet. I'll just nod at the appropriate moments," Dave said.

They left the building like a merry band of misfits and walked to the bar across the street and down a block. A few people stopped Anne and told her the show was well done. Anne Counterman smiled politely and thought about how nice it would be to live in a world where no one talked all the time, where every instance of public record didn't have to be deciphered and discussed, a place where you lived your life and didn't talk about it. The silence was going to be beautiful.

THE PERFECT VALENTINE: EROTIC LESBIAN VALENTINE STORIES edited by Barbara Johnson and Therese Szymanski—from Bella After Dark. 320 pp. Stories from the hottest writers around. 1-59493-061-9 $14.95

MURDER AT RANDOM by Claire McNab. 200 pp. The Sixth Denise Cleever Thriller. Denise realizes the fate of thousands is in her hands. 1-59493-047-3 $12.95

THE TIDES OF PASSION by Diana Tremain Braund. 240 pp. Will Susan be able to hold it all together and find the one woman who touches her soul? 1-59493-048-1 $12.95

JUST LIKE THAT by Karin Kallmaker. 240 pp. Disliking each other—and everything they stand for—even before they meet, Toni and Syrah find feelings can change, just like that. 1-59493-025-2 $12.95

WHEN FIRST WE PRACTICE by Therese Szymanski. 200 pp. Brett and Allie are once again caught in the middle of murder and intrigue. 1-59493-045-7 $12.95

REUNION by Jane Frances. 240 pp. Cathy Braithwaite seems to have it all: good looks, money and a thriving accounting practice . . . 1-59493-046-5 $12.95

BELL, BOOK & DYKE: NEW EXPLOITS OF MAGICAL LESBIANS by Kallmaker, Watts, Johnson and Szymanski. 360 pp. Reluctant witches, tempting spells, and skyclad beauties—delve into the mysteries of love, lust and power in this quartet of novellas. 1-59493-023-6 $14.95

ARTIST'S DREAM by Gerri Hill. 320 pp. When Cassie meets Luke Winston, she can no longer deny her attraction to women . . . 1-59493-042-2 $12.95

NO EVIDENCE by Nancy Sanra. 240 pp. Private Investigator Tally McGinnis once again returns to the horror filled world of a serial killer. 1-59493-043-04 $12.95

WHEN LOVE FINDS A HOME by Megan Carter. 280 pp. What will it take for Anna and Rona to find their way back to each other again? 1-59493-041-4 $12.95

MEMORIES TO DIE FOR by Adrian Gold. 240 pp. Rachel attempts to avoid her attraction to the charms of Anna Sigurdson . . . 1-59493-038-4 $12.95

SILENT HEART by Claire McNab. 280 pp. Exotic lesbian romance.
1-59493-044-9 $12.95

MIDNIGHT RAIN by Peggy J. Herring. 240 pp. Bridget McBee is determined to find the woman who saved her life. 1-59493-021-X $12.95

THE MISSING PAGE A Brenda Strange Mystery by Patty G. Henderson. 240 pp. Brenda investigates her client's murder . . .   1-59493-004-X $12.95

WHISPERS ON THE WIND by Frankie J. Jones. 240 pp. Dixon thinks she and her best friend, Elizabeth Colter, would make the perfect couple . . .   1-59493-037-6 $12.95

CALL OF THE DARK: EROTIC LESBIAN TALES OF THE SUPERNATURAL edited by Therese Szymanski—from Bella After Dark. 320 pp.   1-59493-040-6 $14.95

A TIME TO CAST AWAY A Helen Black Mystery by Pat Welch. 240 pp. Helen stops by Alice's apartment—only to find the woman dead . . .   1-59493-036-8 $12.95

DESERT OF THE HEART by Jane Rule. 224 pp. The book that launched the most popular lesbian movie of all time is back.   1-1-59493-035-X $12.95

THE NEXT WORLD by Ursula Steck. 240 pp. Anna's friend Mido is threatened and eventually disappears . . .   1-59493-024-4 $12.95

CALL SHOTGUN by Jaime Clevenger. 240 pp. Kelly gets pulled back into the world of private investigation . . .   1-59493-016-3 $12.95

52 PICKUP by Bonnie J. Morris and E.B. Casey. 240 pp. 52 hot, romantic tales—one for every Saturday night of the year.   1-59493-026-0 $12.95

GOLD FEVER by Lyn Denison. 240 pp. Kate's first love, Ashley, returns to their home town, where Kate now lives . . .   1-1-59493-039-2 $12.95

RISKY INVESTMENT by Beth Moore. 240 pp. Lynn's best friend and roommate needs her to pretend Chris is his fiancé. But nothing is ever easy.   1-59493-019-8 $12.95

HUNTER'S WAY by Gerri Hill. 240 pp. Homicide detective Tori Hunter is forced to team up with the hot-tempered Samantha Kennedy.   1-59493-018-X $12.95

CAR POOL by Karin Kallmaker. 240 pp. Soft shoulders, merging traffic and slippery when wet . . . Anthea and Shay find love in the car pool.   1-59493-013-9 $12.95

NO SISTER OF MINE by Jeanne G'Fellers. 240 pp. Telepathic women fight to coexist with a patriarchal society that wishes their eradication.   ISBN 1-59493-017-1 $12.95

ON THE WINGS OF LOVE by Megan Carter. 240 pp. Stacie's reporting career is on the rocks. She has to interview bestselling author Cheryl, or else!   ISBN 1-59493-027-9 $12.95

WICKED GOOD TIME by Diana Tremain Braund. 224 pp. Does Christina need Miki as a protector . . . or want her as a lover?   ISBN 1-59493-031-7 $12.95

THOSE WHO WAIT by Peggy J. Herring. 240 pp. Two brilliant sisters—in love with the same woman!   ISBN 1-59493-032-5 $12.95

ABBY'S PASSION by Jackie Calhoun. 240 pp. Abby's bipolar sister helps turn her world upside down, so she must decide what's most important.   ISBN 1-59493-014-7 $12.95

PICTURE PERFECT by Jane Vollbrecht. 240 pp. Kate is reintroduced to Casey, the daughter of an old friend. Can they withstand Kate's career?   ISBN 1-59493-015-5 $12.95

PAPERBACK ROMANCE by Karin Kallmaker. 240 pp. Carolyn falls for tall, dark and . . . female . . . in this classic lesbian romance.   ISBN 1-59493-033-3 $12.95

DAWN OF CHANGE by Gerri Hill. 240 pp. Susan ran away to find peace in remote Kings Canyon—then she met Shawn . . .   ISBN 1-59493-011-2 $12.95

DOWN THE RABBIT HOLE by Lynne Jamneck. 240 pp. Is a killer holding a grudge against FBI Agent Samantha Skellar?   ISBN 1-59493-012-0 $12.95

SEASONS OF THE HEART by Jackie Calhoun. 240 pp. Overwhelmed, Sara saw only one way out—leaving . . . ISBN 1-59493-030-9 $12.95

TURNING THE TABLES by Jessica Thomas. 240 pp. The 2nd Alex Peres Mystery. *From ghosties and ghoulies and long leggity beasties* . . . ISBN 1-59493-009-0 $12.95

FOR EVERY SEASON by Frankie Jones. 240 pp. Andi, who is investigating a 65-year-old murder, meets Janice, a charming district attorney . . . ISBN 1-59493-010-4 $12.95

LOVE ON THE LINE by Laura DeHart Young. 240 pp. Kay leaves a younger woman behind to go on a mission to Alaska . . . will she regret it? ISBN 1-59493-008-2 $12.95

UNDER THE SOUTHERN CROSS by Claire McNab. 200 pp. Lee, an American travel agent, goes down under and meets Australian Alex, and the sparks fly under the Southern Cross. ISBN 1-59493-029-5 $12.95

SUGAR by Karin Kallmaker. 240 pp. Three women want sugar from Sugar, who can't make up her mind. ISBN 1-59493-001-5 $12.95

FALL GUY by Claire McNab. 200 pp. 16th Detective Inspector Carol Ashton Mystery. ISBN 1-59493-000-7 $12.95

ONE SUMMER NIGHT by Gerri Hill. 232 pp. Johanna swore to never fall in love again—but then she met the charming Kelly . . . ISBN 1-59493-007-4 $12.95

TALK OF THE TOWN TOO by Saxon Bennett. 181 pp. Second in the series about wild and fun loving friends. ISBN 1-931513-77-5 $12.95

LOVE SPEAKS HER NAME by Laura DeHart Young. 170 pp. Love and friendship, desire and intrigue, spark this exciting sequel to *Forever and the Night*. ISBN 1-59493-002-3 $12.95

TO HAVE AND TO HOLD by Peggy J. Herring. 184 pp. By finally letting down her defenses, will Dorian be opening herself to a devastating betrayal? ISBN 1-59493-005-8 $12.95

WILD THINGS by Karin Kallmaker. 228 pp. Dutiful daughter Faith has met the perfect man. There's just one problem: she's in love with his sister. ISBN 1-931513-64-3 $12.95

SHARED WINDS by Kenna White. 216 pp. Can Emma rebuild more than just Lanny's marina? ISBN 1-59493-006-6 $12.95

THE UNKNOWN MILE by Jaime Clevenger. 253 pp. Kelly's world is getting more and more complicated every moment. ISBN 1-931513-57-0 $12.95

TREASURED PAST by Linda Hill. 189 pp. A shared passion for antiques leads to love. ISBN 1-59493-003-1 $12.95

SIERRA CITY by Gerri Hill. 284 pp. Chris and Jesse cannot deny their growing attraction . . . ISBN 1-931513-98-8 $12.95

ALL THE WRONG PLACES by Karin Kallmaker. 174 pp. Sex and the single girl—Brandy is looking for love and usually she finds it. Karin Kallmaker's first *After Dark* erotic novel. ISBN 1-931513-76-7 $12.95

WHEN THE CORPSE LIES A Motor City Thriller by Therese Szymanski. 328 pp. Butch bad-girl Brett Higgins is used to waking up next to beautiful women she hardly knows. Problem is, this one's dead. ISBN 1-931513-74-0 $12.95

GUARDED HEARTS by Hannah Rickard. 240 pp. Someone's reminding Alyssa about her secret past, and then she becomes the suspect in a series of burglaries. ISBN 1-931513-99-6 $12.95